tredition®

www.tredition.de

AF203504

Christoffer Krug

More and More

www.tredition.de

© 2020 Christoffer Krug

Verlag und Druck: tredition GmbH, Halenreie 40-44, 22359 Hamburg

ISBN
Paperback: 978-3-347-06521-5
Hardcover: 978-3-347-06522-2
e-Book: 978-3-347-06523-9

Christoffer Krug
More and More

a novel

About the author:

Christoffer Krug was born in Cologne in 1979. He worked as a cleaner, roadie, paramedic, studied medicine in Giessen and New Delhi and works as a doctor. He was editor of the magazine "in weiß" and writes poems and children's books in addition to novels. The father of three lives in Giessen.

More books by Christoffer Krug:

"Come on, paint me a wound", Poems 2010

"Paul sagt AAAHHH", Children's book 2018

"Bevor wir verglühen," Tales 2019

"Das Herz ist auch nur ein Muskel", Poems 2020

Editing: Stephanie Jana

Ben Regan, Elizabeth Regan

www.lektorat-stilsicher.de

1st English Edition 2020

Set from the Bembo Regular

Distribution: tredition.de
ISBN: 978-3-347-06521-5

Bibliographic information of the German National Library: Deutsche Bibliothek lists this publication in the German National Bibliography; detailed bibliographic data is available on the Internet at http://dnb.d-nb.de.

Maybe for Biti Mohanti

Climb the mountains
or descend into the valley,
go to the ends of the earth
or around your house:
you only ever meet yourself
on the streets of Chance.

Maurice Maeterlinck

Frankfurt am Main, Airport 07:06 pm

It smells rancid. I'm on a plane. A puddle of saliva is on my headrest. I must have fallen asleep. Dinner is served. The flight attendants push the catering trolley through the far too narrow aisles. The trolleys are made of baked dough, they bump against the edges and crumble a little further apart at every narrow spot in the aisle. The flight attendants communicate with each other with duck calls, but the chief steward answers with a kazoo. What's going on here?

We're flying through turbulence. When I go to the bathroom, I see a member of the flight crew tied up in the rear of the plane. She was tied to the toilet door with strawberry strings and unrolled liquorice snails, so that I find it difficult to open the door. The toilet is surprisingly spacious. I wash my hands and sit down in a chair hanging from the ceiling. Single drops of water run down the sink and fall to the floor. The ground slowly dissolves.

Now I see through everything. First of all, the plane is made of sugar icing. Secondly: there's a terrorist on board. I'm going to crash into first class and try to expose him. I succeed immediately. It's the SENATOR.

He was already standing in a corner, had opened his pants and just wants to start peeing. I jump up behind him, poke my outstretched index finger in his side and call out: "I've got you figured out SENATOR: You want to pee a huge hole in the sugar plane wall and make us all crash!

The other passengers stare at me and nod thought-fully. The SENATOR closes his pants and sits down again. I have prevented the accident.

Return

A person can recognize hundreds of smells during a lifetime and store many individual scents in his memory for the rest of his life. In my head, the number of smells that I have smelled and accumulated in my life so far has at least doubled in the recent months.

Shit, sweat, dust, spices, disease, poverty, garbage, cows, tea, monkeys, cigarettes, the back of an elephant.

The smells are all on me and they are also in me. Under my arms it smells like cardamom and curry, my clothes smell like the street dust of a city of millions. And the moment the airplane door opens and the dry, cold wind blows the autumn air into my face, I know that I have come back. It smells different, somehow stale, the air here has no smell of its own. It smells sterile, not of laughter, not of life, not of suffering and not of love. The old, fat Germany simply smells of nothing.

I collect my things, stuff my MP3 player into my backpack, put on my worn-out sneakers and search the floor under the seat to make sure I don't leave anything behind. The last 45 minutes on this plane were like time travel back to the 1970s. The replacement plane from London to Frankfurt is an older model. Outside probably well maintained, but inside it is completely in orange and brown. The carpet has orange circles with black dots and looks like it has 100s' of eyes. In this way the plane is the perfect backdrop for the scraps of thoughts that have been circling around in my head for hours. I am back in Germany. Actually I should be happy or relieved. I am not. No one is expecting me here, and so I don't have high expectations of my own return.

My left arm is not usable and hangs in a small noose. If I move it too often, it immediately starts throbbing again. The fingers that stick out at the front of the bandage are red, warm and slightly swollen. In Delhi the bandage had been white for a few minutes, now it is ash grey.

I've been up for hours. In Delhi I almost had to fight for my boarding pass in a small turmoil at the counter to even get a return flight. Now I am infinitely tired.

I did not really miss Germany and my hometown Hamburg. It is said that the hungry always sense food pleasantly in their nostrils, while the satiated feel aversion. When I breathe in the humid and cold autumn air, I almost feel sick.

Slowly the plane empties, I stop in an alcove and wait so that I don't have to be bumped into by anybody in the corridor. The painkillers are used up, and every active or passive movement of my arm immediately sends pain impulses to my brain to remind me of all my mistakes and clumsiness. I have to find a pharmacy quickly and get the strongest possible remedy.

My crumpled passport lies lost in the big hands of the Immigration official, who leafs through it indifferently back and forth. He holds the passport up and his gaze oscillates between my photo on the first page and my face. He sighs audibly, closes the passport and pushes it over the counter. As I leave, I watch from the corner of my eye as he wonders about the red colour on his fingers and rubs them suspiciously. I have almost passed the passport control box when the side door opens again and an official tells me to turn around. In his gaze I read:

You know exactly why!

A couple behind me starts whispering.

They want me to show my passport again.

"Surely you realize that your I.D. is a federal document! How did the paint get in here?"

I shrug my shoulders. I don't feel like explaining something I know they wouldn't understand anyway. I can hear the man behind me explaining in a teacher-like voice to his companion that in some countries it is even forbidden to stain banknotes and that you can be arrested if you do not treat your passport well.

My passport's almost falling apart.

His companion giggles excitedly, and when I turn to her, she gives me a pitiful but stern look with her arrogant eyes. Let them arrest me. I don't care if they arrest me.

Of course they'll let me go after the lecture. The baggage carousel is already making its rounds when I arrive. My luggage is shrunk down to a little grey duffel bag. Most of what I thought was so important was lost in India. It feels so good to travel with light luggage.

In the arrival terminal I find a pharmacy and buy a box of tablets. I take two of them still in the shop and swallow them laboriously without water. The pharmacist stares at me as if I were a junkie pushing heroin in her shop.

I hardly know my way around the station at Frankfurt Airport, but the infallible German signs with their beautiful, clear and factual inscriptions show me the way to the long-distance train station a few floors down. Everything is modern, everything is clean, many things shine. I walk through the tubular halls straight on and on, like a hamster lost in a gigantic pneumatic tube system. How does someone feel who has never seen all this in its glittering splendour and sober functionality before?

I just want to sleep. Standard question for testing depressive tendencies: Do you sometimes have the desire to fall asleep and not wake up again? Answer: I wouldn't care *if* I *could* just sleep.

The queue at the ticket counter consists of three people. A businessman with a grey coat over his suit and briefcase looks at his lush Omega Seamaster and blows the air between his teeth in a stressed way. I have to grin to myself. I got used to much longer human que. They are in themselves an immeasurable luxury. A sign of discipline and order in chaos. From the type of queues you can tell the nationality of the people. I have to grin again when I think of how the lady at the ticket counter would react to a siege of 100 men from India with similar moustaches.

My scratched Visa card pays for the ticket to Hamburg. 106 Euros for the luxury of a four-hour and five-minute trip. It doesn't get any faster.

I am cold. The skin on my hands is flaking, and for the first time I start to feel dirty in this environment. When I go to the toilet, I look in the mirror again after a long time. I might as well hold the cover of some magazine in front of my face. Never did I expect to become such a stranger to myself. Only now do I understand the looks of people on the plane, at the counters, in the pharmacy. I look strange. My face is brown. But it does not have the average tan of a nice holiday, it looks leathery, shiny and tanned. Areas of skin with old mosquito bites on my neck have been left lighter. My eyes look like they were made up with an eyeliner and the cheekbones have become more prominent. But the most impressive thing for me is that the man in the mirror has a beard. When I used to stroke my face, I always felt a thin layer of fluff covering my chin and upper lip. But now everything is overgrown, I can no longer see any free skin between my upper lip and neck. With both hands I scoop water into my face. I don't dry myself off, but go straight out into the cold, draughty platform tunnel. The piercing cold in my face revives me briefly.

My mind is racing, the painkillers are starting to work. The gradual fading of the throbbing pain has almost a euphoric effect on me. The ICE *Stuttgart* enters quickly and stops almost silently, without making squeaking noises when braking. I involuntarily have to think of something gentle. The gentlest things I can imagine at the moment are Alex and Nora. Alex and Nora are my friends. I helped them, and they were there for me. That's what friends do for each other. Positive energy doesn't get lost. I hope they're okay now. They really deserve it.

I choose a nice compartment and hope that I will remain alone. The linen bag is standing on the seat next to me, heaving it up on the luggage rack, I don't see myself in a position to do so. In this way I can lean sideways against it. With the correspondingly tightly stuffed contents, it conveys the feeling of a big, strong friend to whom one can lean on calmly.

The train starts slowly, hardly noticeable.

Never before have I felt that my thoughts could no longer obey me. My brain and all my memories are like a film reel that got tangled up when I played it. Individual, faltering images appear on the screen, but everything is completely blurred by the careless efforts of the projectionist to thread the film roll back in correctly as quickly as possible before the cinema audience goes on a rampage and demands its money back. The film has three main actors. Two of them are really important. The third one not so much.

I'm the third.

I feel in the pocket of my dirty fleece jacket and find the iPod. The screen doesn't work anymore, but if I try around long enough I can still activate the random function. I lean back against my luggage and close my eyes. There is something good about blindly operating an iPod with a broken display: chance is then my DJ, and he almost always shows excellent taste in finding the right songs for my moods.

Play and *Rewind* are close together. Just like my life. The music starts. The memories of the most moving moments rewind. The journey begins again.

First comes a simple bass run. I imagine the band getting on stage in the fog, with the lights off, one by one. The guitar is added, the distortion is already turned up to the limit, but the thumb still dampens most of the strings. The drums start with the snare and get louder and louder. Everybody plays in the same rhythm. Only two bars. Three people stand together on stage in the dark, they understand each other without words. It only takes one look at each other, and in the next moment, when the spotlights are completely turned on, the full sound blasts out of the amplifiers. The first song line, which can only be screamed because all the accumulated energy is discharged at the same time, sounds through the headphones:

Is that a leaf in your hair, or the autumn that's inside me?

The air smells of seaweed. It's warm and I'm sitting on a harbor wall. My legs dangle down. When the water comes in a small wave, it gently touches the soles of my bare feet. A ferry slowly drives backwards into the pier. The tailgate opens and shows the interior. Everything is pink. The walls are covered with plush cushions, the floor completely covered with thick mattresses. Asian looking helpers tie the ferry to the ramp with thick ropes. In doing so, they often stumble, because the soft upholstery always gives way and the workers sink in. A delivery van drives backwards up to the ramp. The door is opened and at the back a small pink elephant trots out. The elephant trumpets loudly but becomes quieter and quieter as the loading hatch closes. The ferry slowly departs. My feet are completely washed over by a wave.

Nora

I had heard from many people that Indian Airlines was not exactly the most reliable airline. At least it was the cheapest for the outward flight. I was already four hours late. Two hours were still ahead of me, according to the big ads.

Airports have always held a certain fascination for me. They are hubs of extensive air connections that span the whole world in large networks. This is where everything comes together. Travelers, seekers and: escapees.

My little notebook lay unfolded on my legs. Meanwhile I sat cross-legged for so long that my feet started to tingle. I put the backpack behind my head and stretched out completely. For the hundredth time I opened the e-mail that I had saved as a file on my desktop: a scanned document, impressive letterhead, clear words in the cover letter. None other than Johann Wolfgang von Goethe looked down at me confidently from his emblem frame. The director of the institute in New Delhi had expressed himself more than eclectically, probably he had to write like that when comparing himself with Goethe.

"Dear Mr. Kemper,

With regard to your numerous letters of the last months, it is a great pleasure to inform you that you have been accepted as guest editor. Your employment

is initially on a trial basis and is limited to six months..."
- and so on

My brilliant plan had worked. For weeks I had been pestering the institute in New Delhi with my application letters. I didn't care that in the end it was probably only my father's letter of recommendation that made the job easy. Even during my journalism studies I had wished for nothing more than to work abroad and, at best, to be on the spot and report when history was being written somewhere. The prospect of helping the Institute in New Delhi to represent Germany abroad was not quite what I had imagined, but it was at least a start. I knew that I would live in a magnificent city.

Other people, other food, other thoughts.

For four months I had been waiting to leave. I had had my exams in my pocket for a year, and slowly I felt the subliminal pressure from my parents to finally stand on my own two feet.

The idea of a regular reporter's job in some cramped office in Germany, which is the same every day and probably boring without exception, frightened me. Up to now, the important course of my life had always set itself. To call it coincidence would probably have been too much. If I believed in fate, it would probably be the reason why I was now sitting and waiting here.

Because sitting, waiting and doing nothing wasn't my kind of thing, I started writing texts and columns about Germany very early. I knew that I would be given enough freedom on the spot to choose the topics. Over the weeks a nice number of articles had already accumulated. In my mind I saw myself briefly visiting the institute in the morning and delivering some small proof of my commitment, and then exploring the city and the country from noon on. Of course I would participate in the usual socialising appointments, but that would be it. For me it was only a means to an end. Paid accommodation, a small salary and half a year in India. So my plan was about to be implemented which I found brilliant.

If you had to choose a sound to go with that feeling of wanderlust, for me it was the rattling sound of the name changes on the departure boards: *Kuala Lumpur, Hong Kong, Cape Town, Taipei.*

These names have fascinated me ever since I was a child and had visited this airport frequently with my uncle. Here you could meet people in turbans, old men with long white beards in caftans, or tall Texans with cowboy hats and boots. Even a short stay in the terminal was enough to sniff the air of the big, wide world.

About 200 passengers sat at the gate, most of them resting in themselves and quietly, a few individuals in ties and suits walking up and down nervously.

Cell phone sounds. Echoes of their voices.

It was only 11 o'clock in the morning and many of the business people had sat down at a bar. They were drinking Bitburger. I watched them and after thinking about it for a while I decided to buy one. But I felt so stupid and observed that I just chugged the beer and then took my place on the floor again. I had quickly counted the money and put it on the table. The waitress stared at me in surprise.

A short, buddy-buddy hug of beer.

Slightly intoxicated at 11:00 a.m. Not too bad, actually.

Diagonally opposite sat a woman who was about 30 years old and had long brown hair. I had noticed her when I checked in. Of the few Europeans standing in line, she was the only one not wearing trekking trousers or a tropical functional shirt. She was simply dressed quite normally. Her legs were in slightly worn jeans, and she was wearing worn out blue sneakers and a green fleece jacket.

She looked very natural – and that made her pretty.

When she looked in my direction again, our eyes met.

Strange familiarity.

She had a narrow face with fine features, her eyes looked tired. As hand luggage she only had a thin, tube-shaped, waterproof bag, like the ones used for canoeing. When she noticed that our eyes met, a short smile flew over her face, then she turned her head away again and immersed herself in her book.

Until the whispering voice of the flight attendants finally called for boarding, I had fallen asleep twice. Three quarters of the queue at the gate was already in the belly of the plane when I got up and lined up too. I stared straight ahead.

There she was again. Right in front of me. She was reading and, absorbed in her reading, pushed her bag forward with her foot. Then she briefly closed her book and looked around.

My eyes fell first on the book cover, then on her. I smiled, and without thinking twice, I said:

"You like *Gonzo*?"

She looked at me at a loss.

"You read Hunter S. Thompson." And I pointed to her book.

"My favorite writer."

Now she smiled too.

"Yeah, I just started, I don't know what you mean by Gonzo."

She showed me with her finger that she had only read about ten pages.

"But you're right, the preface alone is unique"

She turned the pages over a few times. In the meantime, we were just about to enter the gate. Again she took the book and said:

"He compares writing to sex. It's only fun for people who don't *have to* do it. "

I replied amused:

"I know, and then he writes in comparison, old whores don't have much to laugh about."

Now she smiled. I had to laugh too.

"There is of course a great truth in it," I said with a humorous undertone.

Actually, it was completely true and was true for me in any case. I hated having to write and under pressure

I mostly produced only incoherent texts that even I wouldn't have wanted to read a second time. Not exactly the best quality for a journalist.

Then she stood in front of the gate and was asked for her boarding card. While her ticket was scanned, she turned back to me.

"Have a safe flight.

"Thank you, you too. And have fun reading!"

She smiled and went on the plane.

Go far away to come back later and see what has changed.

I thought to myself briefly when I crossed the threshold of the 747 and was greeted by the Indian flight attendants.

Would anything be able to change at all?

I didn't have to squeeze far through the corridors. At the check-in I had used all my powers of persuasion and begged for a place at the front by the emergency exit. I stowed my backpack, sat down and looked forward to eight hours of perfect legroom and a hopefully restful nap.

When I had just settled in, a mildly smiling Indian stewardess came to me. Behind her stood a young woman with a cute, very small child in her arms. He could hardly be more than a year old and already wore little gold bracelets around his wrists.

I was clearly looking forward to it too soon. I was supposed to switch seats. Given the small family idyll, who would have started a discussion? Smiling a little sourly, I collected my things again. 12 A against 56 F. I did not like the rear part of large airplanes. Somehow I always had a queasy feeling when I had to sit in the back.

The machine did not smell like other planes. There was a spicy smell in the air from the very first minute. Cardamom, curry and people, that sort of thing.

Magazines were displayed on an open hand luggage compartment.

From a distance I saw the typical yellow of the National Geographic Magazine and was happy. Just as I was about to take the last magazine, an overweight, bearded gentleman with a yellow turban pushed in front and took all the issues. He also took the meagre remains of the newspapers, which would have interested me. When I finally reached into the box, there was only one women's magazine left. *12 hairstyle trends in summer, big knit extra, designing glitter pumps myself.* I took a deep breath. Well then, maybe better than nothing.

I had hardly taken my eyes off the top bar to read the seat numbers. When I reached 56, I looked down. She looked up at me at the same moment. I had the feeling I was blushing without knowing exactly why.

She dropped her book. Her eyes were slate gray.

"So, you like reading about hairstyles and knitting?"

I looked over to her shelf on the back of the seat, where she had a copy of every available newspaper and magazine.

"No wonder you hoard all the newspapers!" I said that in a casual way.

She smiled briefly and read on in her book.

When I had stowed the backpack and settled in, I held out my hand to her.

"MORITZ."

She looked up from the book and took my hand. Her handshake was firmer than I expected. It was as if we had to make something clear from the start that I didn't know what it was.

"NORA."

She kept holding my hand in hers while she mischievously threw in something:

"Isn't it true that if by chance you meet three times in a row, drink invitations must be expressed?"

I smiled.

"That's right, I'll get you a tomato juice right now!"

After one and a half hours in the air we had our first meal. Chicken curry with rice, what else. In the meantime we hadn't talked much. Nora read in her Gonzo book and I read in a National Geographic, which she had given me before with a compassionate gesture.

In the meantime I was even a little grateful to the stewardess for my forced move. Nora was nice and I felt comfortable in her presence.

When the food was in front of us, I struggled with the welded plastic cutlery and tried to get the knife and fork out. Nora put her book aside and opened the aluminium cover of her bowl. Then she calmly reached into her food with her hand and mixed the curry sauce with the rice with her outstretched forefinger and then stuffed a handful of it into her mouth. Chewing, she looked at me. A small splash of sauce was splashed on her cheek like a beauty mark. There was something triumphant in her gaze. Again I felt I was blushing in front of her for reasons I didn't understand myself. While using the plastic cutlery at dinner I felt stupid.

"You've been to India, haven't you?"

"Yes, for a while. You haven't, have you?"

Although I did not know if she was interested, I started to tell her about my plans in India. She listened rather unimpressed. Her eyes once wandered up and down on me. Then she said determinedly:

"Sounds to me like you're running away from something."

Without saying another word, she then climbed over me and left me alone with my curry and her clear words.

When she came back, I had finished and the trays had already been cleared. She stood in front of me for a moment and put one hand on her hip. Then she tied her hair behind her head and bent down to me.

Every movement a flawless staging.

She approached my head and said, almost in a whisper:

"Why were you staring at me like that at the counter a few hours ago?"

What kind of question was that? I couldn't get out of the shameful feeling.

"I wasn't staring at you. I was just kind of, uh, noticing you."

She laughed. In any case, she didn't seem to be angry, and I guess she didn't take it all that seriously. I relaxed a little.

Nora stood up and stretched out her thin arms in the air, then she asked:

"Do you know *François Truffaut*?"

"That French director?"

"Have you ever seen any of his films?"

"I don't think so."

"You really missed out. There's a great film by him: *The Man Who Loved Women*. I think it's from the '80s."

Her eyes were shining and I had no idea why she was telling me this.

"Well... there's this guy in the movie who's really into women's legs. Wherever women walk around, his first interest is always in the legs, and he's always looking at them. In spite of his odd way he usually gets on quite well with the ladies and he always has some adventures. At some point he writes a book about his affairs. One day he gets hit by a car on the street because he's been staring too much once again."

"This is tragic..."

"Yes, but the end is even more tragic because he is then in hospital and finally dies when he accidentally pulls out his own IV tube. But all this only happens because he bends over too far to see the nurse's legs!"

I couldn't help smiling. She climbed over me again, as a matter of course, to get to her seat, saying softly:

"Well, some men are rigid."

"But I wasn't staring!" I burst out in indignation.

"Whatever you say, now you know where staring can lead you."

Was I wrong, or had Nora winked at me in that last sentence?

She had a real talent for charming me with everything she said. But at the same time, she made me feel very stupid. An abstruse mixture of two opposing emotions.

"So why *are you* going to India? To find meaning, a yoga retreat or a vacation?"

Already while these words came over my lips in a somewhat succinct tone, I had the vague feeling of putting my foot in it.

Nora looked at me very seriously. Then the stern expression left her face for a moment and she said:

"Not quite."

"Then what?"

"I'm trying to find my father."

I swallowed briefly.

"Excuse me. Will you explain it to me?"

For a brief moment I was ashamed of my obvious curiosity, but then I remembered her brazen behaviour from just now. Besides, a healthy portion of curiosity was part of my job, why not start right here? I looked at her expectantly.

Nora hesitated.

"I'll have to go a long way on this one. Are you sure you want to do this?"

"Sure."

I nodded my head for sure.

She shrugged her shoulders indifferently but then folded her table up and pulled her legs up to her body.

Then she put her chin on her knees and began to talk in a calm tone. The words came over her lips so fluently that one got the impression that this was not the first time she told the story.

"My parents met at this university. In the sixties my father studied medicine in Berlin, my mother became a teacher. The summer they graduated, they had everything else in mind than to start a career and a normal bourgeois life in Germany. It was 1967, the *Summer of Love* had begun. Friends from America told my parents about the *Human Be In in* San Francisco. That summer, my father memorized entire speeches by Timothy Leary about people's right to free access to mind-expanding drugs.

Everything was questioned, completely new ways had to be found. In a psylocibin frenzy in a Kreuzberg flat share, with their American friends and Jefferson Airplane in their ears, my parents therefore came up with the most sensible plan for them: to buy a motorcycle and leave Europe to go to spiritual places, the places of true and pure life, the home of their only role models.

My parents had to go to India for this. In 1968 they both started to follow the Hippie Trail by motorbike. Sheepskin jackets and wind goggles as well as a small tent helped them with incredible luck to survive the inhuman strains on their journey via Istanbul and Tehran to Kabul. Well, and probably a huge amount of dope too."

Nora reached for her backpack and pulled out a wrinkled envelope from which she pulled a battered black and white photo. The photograph showed a bearded young man. Eyes brightly surrounded, while the rest of the face was deeply tanned. Next to him stood a small woman in tattered jeans and army jacket in front of a tent.

I looked at the photo for a while. It was a nice picture, very expressive. Full of youth. There was an immediate resemblance to Nora.

"The motorcycle became useless over time and was unceremoniously given to a laughing Pashtun. From Kabul to Goa was only a manageable, short distance compared to the entire route.

My parents took the train, and hitchhiked the rest of the way until they arrived in Goa. They decided to stay there for a while. Goa seemed to be the perfect place for my parents to start their planned family. My father started to operate a rubber machine with a Goanese in a small hut on the beach. With it they could pay for the most basic necessities of life. Meanwhile, my mother was sitting on the beach weaving colourful cloths in her small community. She simply wanted to give herself over to her undemanding selfishness and live out her psychedelic family dream."

Nora laughed bitterly, then she went on.

"My mother loved the free life. My father began to have doubts about the whole concept of free love. Making possessive claims on each other's bodies displeased my mother. I was less than 4 weeks old when she slept with a Dane on a full moon night on the beach in the monsoon rain. My father knew this, but secretly hoped we could stay together as a family."

Nora went on. Excitement and anger were in her voice.

"But she kept fucking her way through the entire commune. My father was so affected and hurt that one night, when I was about three months old, he packed his companion's small bus with 150 kg of raw rubber and left the woman he loved and his daughter, who would never really remember him. My mother now had a child, but the late, very pervasive awareness of having lost the man of her life forced her to search for more and deeper knowledge. She told herself that she still had to find the meaning of her life. A man who called himself Bhagwan Shree Rajneesh seemed to be the right guide on this messed up journey of self-discovery. My mother took me and the Dane and brought us to Poona."

In her words, mockery competed with melancholy.

"I turned six years old, spoke Hindi quite well by now and spent most of the time in the Ashram with small groups of children where I could do everything I liked. There were no supervisors. My mother didn't care much about me because she preferred to spend most of her time naked in extensive group meditations.

"A social revolution had to be preceded by a sexual revolution!"

Nora rolled her eyes. Then she took a small water bottle and took a sip. As she did so, she looked out the window and shook her head over her own thoughts.

"There was this guy in one of the seminars my mom went to. He claimed he'd invented an apparatus that could isolate life energy in the form of tiny bubbles. My mother had even bought such an 'accumulator' from him, where the energy could be used for therapeutic purposes. Can you imagine such bullshit?

I nodded my understanding.

"The rest of the time my mother and the other Bhagwan devotees took care of the maintenance of the ashram. Shortly after my sixth birthday events started to happen and my usual world with the orange robes, the many naked people and the whole carnival environment collapsed from one day to the next.

"What happened?"

"You won't believe it, but sometimes the most banal coincidences lead to everything changing!

The Dane was caught smuggling opium and disappeared, without ever reappearing, in some prison. Besides, I had washed my hair all alone that day. A friend of my mother had given me a small shrink-wrapped shampoo bag. Since such articles were rather rare in the Ashram, I was naturally very curious and pressed the whole package on my head at once. After my hair had dried, I waited with my mother in front of the Buddha Hall for the terribly boring weekly speech of Bhagwan. A long queue had formed in front of the door, and just before we could cross the threshold, a watchman bent down to me and sniffed my hair. The guard immediately pulled a face and stood in the way of my mother. Due to an unfortunate chain of misunderstandings, a few unfavourable bumps and the quick-tempered behaviour of the guards, we were thrown out of the ashram very quickly and not very politely. The head guru had a fine nose and could not bear it if someone perfumed listened to his lectures. This failed trial, which had led to my mother's expulsion from paradise, quite wounded her.

Even after returning to Germany shortly afterwards, I was never allowed to use shampoos or deodorants. For years after that all body care products caused reproach for my mother."

The on-board lighting in the plane had been switched off in the meantime, a film was running on the small monitors above us. The roar of the engines had something sleepy about it. For a long time I had once again completely lost the feeling for time and my surroundings.

"And what is driving you to find your father after all these years?"

"I need to find him to find out if this is what my life was supposed to be like. I need to find him to find out if it all makes sense."

"And how do you plan to do that? Do you have any contacts?"

She ignored my questions completely and finished her thoughts a little dreamily without looking at me.

"Maybe all of us in this crazy world are being cut in half by our bad experiences. Everyone's always looking for something. Maybe everybody's just looking for his second half!"

"And you're seeking your father because you think he's the second half of your soul?"

"Maybe. Somehow I feel there's a connection. He made my mother happy. I think if he'd stayed, things might have been better. At the same time, I have this feeling that I have to confront him. I want to know why he left me. I have some unfinished business with him, so to speak.

It's like an Italian Western.

Nora's eyes occasionally wandered into the distance. In those moments I thought I could get an impression of how alone she really was.

I told Nora about my father. The well-known journalist, for whom everything became too monotonous, too two-dimensional a few years ago. He had given up his job, bought some film equipment and started to produce self-made documentaries for television. Who let his hair grow longer, suddenly rode a motorcycle, and who a few years ago cheated on my mother with a student who was barely older than me.

We talked in a whisper about parents, about intact relationships and their irreplaceable importance for one's own inner balance. We talked in long sentences, in monologues - and I felt good about it. Then I got tired. Nora sighed once into the newly entered silence and leaned against the window with her pillow. While I fell asleep, a band was singing:

In your mind you build a monument,

with a plaque that says,

what once was and never is,

in a place where no one goes.

Nora's head was on my shoulder. She was fast asleep and her hair smelled of a fruity shampoo. Berries and some of the stuff that gives freshly washed girl's hair that seductive scent. I leaned forward slightly to get a better look at her lips. Her breath smelled good. While trying to inhale her exhaled air, I bent forward too far and she woke up. I thought she would pull her head back immediately, but to my amazement she stayed lying down, turned her head just a little and closed her eyes again. But she did not sleep any further.

"Moritz, what did you dream while you were sleeping?"

"I just fell asleep for a moment, I didn't dream anything." I was *lying*.

The truth is, I kept dreaming very absurd things. Things that were perhaps even great to tell and with which I could reap some laughs. But I didn't feel like it.

"If you could choose a dream that would repeat itself over and over in your life, what would it be?"

Her eyes were still closed. It was dark, and her face was bathed in a faint orange light from the reading lamp in the front seat.

"I don't know... What would *you* wish for in a dream?"

"I used to dream a lot about being one of the *Famous Five* and having crazy adventures."

"On mysterious islands and all that?"

"Exactly!"

I felt her head fall back onto my shoulder.

"In these dreams I always felt very strong and the tension was always very pleasant. So pleasant that now when I have these dreams, I still feel sad and wake up too soon."

Then Nora fell asleep again.

Monotonous jet plane noise. 30000 feet high, 800 kilometers an hour.

Nora was very generous with her affection. I knew this behavior. I'd seen it before. It's usually the way of people who've been alone a lot in their lives.

When I looked at the screen above us again, I was startled. The writing with the small map, on which you could see the position of our plane, changed between Hindi and English. We only had two hours to fly.

Nora had turned to the side and continued dozing.

Had we now arrived at the point where, by exchanging any contact details, people showed each other that they liked each other, or that they were just fooling around?

It felt as if we had just started in Frankfurt. While I was thinking about it, the plane started to descend.

Without me saying anything, Nora whispered next to me:

"Do you believe in that soul mates thing I was talking about earlier?"

"It certainly sounds nice. Yeah, I think I could believe in it. Where will you go when we get to Delhi?"

"I'm going to Goa."

Then we kept quiet. So this is how it would be.

Nora walked beside me up to the passport control. She looked sleepily at the floor, and it seemed as if she was avoiding my gaze.

I was fascinated. Here I stood breathing India, and New Delhi began to inhale me. Nora didn't seem to be impressed by all this. I turned to the exit of the terminal, where a huge crowd of people was huddled. I looked back at the passport control.

I was alone.

Nora had been swallowed up from one second to the next. Her exit was so perfect, she must have planned it in advance. In my jacket pocket I found a crumpled up ball of paper. The paper felt warm when unfolded and was a bit damp. The letters had been written hastily:

"When you run and hide from something, you only run into your fate. It was nice talking to you.

Nora"

Cologne central station, 08:05 pm

I've been scrubbing the wooden deck of a small boat for hours. The planks are rough, my fingers are full of splinters. Joseph Conrad himself is the captain. He's only got one hand and he's always complaining. He can never keep it clean enough. The river has no water. We are driving agonizingly slowly through quicksand. The diesel engines make a tremendous noise to propel the boat slowly forward. Constantly new quicksand swells on to the deck. The sun has burnt my neck. We are transporting several barrels of molasses. The sticky syrup often runs out of the barrels, and when the quicksand falls on it, it makes pretty patterns. Joseph Conrad limps across the deck. Most of the time, however, he sits indoors and writes. In between he comes out to get some of the syrup for his cornflakes. But I never get any. I get scolded all the time.

India

The Indira Gandhi Airport resembled an anthill at eleven o'clock in the morning. It smelled spicy, but above all it smelled of many people. One look was enough to see that the chances of finding anyone here were zero. Indians were sitting on the ground everywhere, many were lying in the corridors on the edge, their luggage protectively built around them. Despite air conditioning, the air was already extremely humid and muggy, and my clothes stuck to my body within minutes.

Mild dizziness. Feels like walking on a swaying ship.

Although most signs were written in English as well as Hindi, I had no idea where to find the exit. With my two backpacks I pushed myself through the crowds to the counter of the airline *Spice Jet*. When I asked about the exit and the taxis the lady at the counter answered me:

"Tike tike," bouncing her head right and left. She was pretty. A red dot between the brows, like a third eye.

She had just answered me "*okay, okay*". Nothing more. Suddenly I just wanted to lie down somewhere and sleep.

At a small ATM I got a bundle of banknotes and stuffed one half of the bundle into my socks and the other half into my belt in a back corner of the airport. Then I joined a small group of turban-wearing Sikhs and arrived at the door.

The heat struck me like a fist on my skull. In front of the main entrance the chaos was even bigger. The air was filled with a yellow mist. It smelled like burnt wood.

Hundreds of men stood behind a small Metal barrier, and when they saw me, they stretched out their arms to pull me by the sleeve and yelled their taxi offers at me. At first glance, they all looked almost the same. They all had pretty black moustaches and wore shirts with two pens in the breast pocket. Inside I was of course considerably overwhelmed by the situation. I just tried to get through to the prepaid taxi stand. Amidst the crowd of angry taxi drivers without a license I was stopped again. I couldn't think of anything better than looking at my fingernails and mumbling - *"tike, tike"* - and moving my head like the *Spice Jet* counter girl.

Pushing and shoving was unavoidable, but so I finally reached the front of the taxi counter, threw a few bills on the counter and named my destination. Despite the large amount of money I didn't get any change back, but I did not care at that moment. I was immediately taken to an old black Ambassador from the 1960s. I pressed my prepaid bill into the driver's hand, pulled the door shut and was delighted to finally be in the taxi.

Pleasantly cool leather seats.

I couldn't estimate the age of the driver, he wore a cloth around his neck with which he regularly wiped his face. He smelled of two things: a sweetish sweat-curry mixture, which I found very pleasant, and of burnt leaves from the small rolled up tobacco leaves he smoked. For a five rupee he handed me one of them to the back and said:

"*Beedie*, good!"

He showed the raised right thumb and gave me matches. I leaned back, sucked on the crumbly stick and blew the stinking smoke through a crack in the window. The Ambassador drove leisurely away from the airport, and a comfortable dizziness pushed me slowly and comfortably into the seat. I had arrived in India, and even though my thoughts were actually still in Germany and on the plane with Nora, New Delhi came noticeably closer to me in large steps.

Although it must have been really bright by this time of day, the streets continued to be bathed in a dull yellowish light, like fog, that allowed a visibility of hardly more than ten metres. Silently we drove along big main roads into the centre of New Delhi. At the roadside I kept seeing cows between big heaps of garbage, with their snouts rummaging through it for food. The traffic increased, and occasionally the cows crossed the streets slowly and smoothly, but this only seemed to hinder the flow of traffic slightly. One simply steered a hair's breadth past the animals. At least in this situation nobody used the horn.

Driving past, I noticed lumpy rolls on the gutter again and again. After a while I realized that these were actually people sleeping at the roadside wrapped in dirty towels.

Like dead bodies.

I stared spellbound from the taxi at this new environment. At intersections and traffic lights where we stopped, my surroundings again stared at me.

Again and again small, terribly mutilated children approached the taxi and tried to stick their hands through the window which I had opened a crack. My driver then turned to me each time and smiled a mild smile with his yellow-red teeth.

We were approaching the centre. The rush hour had taken over the taxi.

Unlike the small motor rickshaws, the little agile taxi was wedged in a gigantic, colourful avalanche of tin with a honking concert. I cranked the window all the way up, but I couldn't turn my gaze away from the side of the road. Bicyclists with trailers on which fruit and red nuts were lying wound their way through the traffic jam. The pavement stopped right at the edge of the road, and from there the dusty, sometimes loamy ground began. Numerous huts made of tin and cardboard lined the roadside between the paved houses. Dirty cloths on sticks had been stretched between them to separate the walls. Everywhere people of different ages sat around small bowls with wood fires and stirred pots. I could make out a pipe that rose out of the earth at an angle from which rusty brown water was running. Men with raised wrap skirts crouched in front of it and pooped on the softened ground. I could smell it all the way to the taxi. A mixture of burning wood, cooked food, two-stroke exhaust, urine, sewage, cow shit and human shit.

Welcome to the jungle.

The institute was located in *Bangla Sahib Road*, not far from the huge circular Connaught Place. But as my taxi driver either did not know the address or did not want to continue, I got out with my two backpacks at Connaught-Place. I was, so to speak, in the touristic centre of the city, but this didn't really give me a good feeling. Where there were tourists, there was mostly trouble and cheating. I had learned this a long time ago on other trips. I did not consider myself a tourist, because I came here to work, but I looked like one.

An Italian couple was arguing in front of me.

Manorial white buildings alternated with modern high-rise buildings to enclose the square in a perfect circle. Here Delhi really looked it's most modern. Without any orientation as to which of the radiating roads was the right one to the institute, I started to dig out the guide book. In this way, of course, I distinguished myself more than anything else as a tourist, and it took hardly a minute before a shoeshine boy offered me his services. Thankfully, I refused the trustful old man and was about to refer to my still very clean shoes, when I looked down at myself and found a big lump of shit on the tip of my shoe. Without waiting for my answer, the cleaner busily began to work on my shoes. While he was doing this, I quickly flipped through my map and quickly found the way to the institute, wondering about the unrestrained grinning looks of the passing Indians. I pressed a ten-rupee note into the shoeshine boy's hand, which immediately led to an embarrassing discussion about more money. So I gave in and handed the old man another ten rupees, then I left the big circle. The cleaner followed me and continued to scold me, after 50 meters he finally let go of me and looked for new customers.

I soon realized that I had chosen the wrong way and had turned off one road too early. On the short way back I could hardly believe my eyes: The shoeshine boy was sneaking in front of me and had hitched himself to an American tourist couple. Behind his back, clearly visible to me, he carried a small bucket with stinking brown contents. With extraordinary dexterity, he quickly put a small spoon into the pot and hurled the contents between the American's legs, where the little lump of poop landed exactly on the shoe. Immediately afterwards the crazy shit thrower spoke to them.

Mister, Mister, Shoeshine.

I totally fell for it. Barely two hours in the city and then this. I didn't feel like getting involved in anything else. The American already pulled out a big bill. I guess anyone who looked like a tourist had to learn the hard way in the beginning.

The institute was housed in an unimposing and modern building. A guard stood at the gate and let me in immediately without any problems. The air conditioner blew icy air into my back, and as soon as the door behind me closed, I started to freeze. I was still wearing my sweaty and sleep drooling T-shirt. In the entrance hall there was a small porter's table, but it was not occupied.

What a nice sterile island.

I found the toilets and squeezed myself into the small room with my backpacks. After I had freshened up a bit, I came back to the foyer with a neat shirt and a tie. I had a hard time with the tie decision. Actually, I did not like ties, but for my highly official registration for work I had to dress decently. Meanwhile, the porter was back at his place and took my luggage for supervision, then I was led through a corridor in the upper floor into a small anteroom. On the way I met some young employees or trainees and greeted them in a friendly way. Everyone was wearing jeans and T-shirts and looked at me in astonishment.

Damn it.

Behind me I could hear her whispering and felt even worse. They were probably laughing.

I waited in a small anteroom. Portrait photographs of the Federal Presidents hung on the walls. While I was wondering why I liked Richard von Weizsäcker the most of all, the side door opened and I was greeted by a man of about 50 years with a bald head, wearing a white shirt. Like most people here, he wore a name tag on which was written: "*Klaus Mordmüller* ".

Exuberantly he shook my hand, whereby he additionally held my elbow with his other one, which was immediately very unpleasant for me.

"So you are Moritz, our most diligent application writer!"

The fact that he immediately said *"our"* in this context was very friendly, but somehow I already had a bad feeling about the greeting.

"I've heard a lot about you from your father."

I nodded briefly. I had been prepared for this sentence and followed his hand movement into his office. As I walked behind him, I had the impression of smelling rosewater. But underneath there was some other smell, something stronger.

Klaus Mordmüller had a large office, the walls were panelled with dark wood on the lower half, and the floor was also made of freshly planed wood. A wide oak desk stood in the middle, and on the walls, for my feeling completely unsuitable for this noble ambience, hung old posters with German city views. Something like that usually hung in classrooms abroad. After the standard sensitivities had been exchanged: flight, first impression of Delhi, the dirt, *yes yes...*, he poured me a glass of water and sat back comfortably in his leather armchair.

"Of course you can call me Klaus! We all see ourselves as one big family here, and since I'm the boss here, I naturally try to keep the hierarchies as flat as possible!"

I smiled, thought, "They are always the worst!", and was flattered. I raised my water glass and said:

"Nice to meet you, Klaus.

In reality, I just got extremely tired and really just wanted to find a room somewhere and sleep. But Klaus started to talk to me about some, as he said, *very important things.* I had expected that now I would get to know details about my tasks, but basically he only talked about himself and his view of what was the task of Germany in India and the whole world. After only a minute I began to nod monotonously and occasionally clear my throat.

Finally, I found a good moment to ask him for suitable accommodation nearby. The desire for a shower and a bed got bigger and bigger. Klaus wrote down the name of a private dormitory on a piece of paper and described the way there in a complicated way. Then he gave me his own telephone number and accompanied me to the door. Again, I noticed the conspicuous and to this man hardly fitting smell of rose water.

Since it was Friday, I should settle in properly and get back to him on Monday, everything else would be discussed then.

Klaus grinned again very winningly and held the door open for me. The small gust of wind it caused, carried this spicy under-smell into my nose again, and when leaving the antechamber it came to my mind: The extremely friendly Klaus Mordmüller simply smelled of – *hashish*.

In the corridor I again met a small group of younger colleagues.

I quickly untied the tie knot and wound up the long tie in my hand. As I came closer, their whispering stopped. I introduced myself politely.

Smile like you mean it.

The looks of the four could not have been more arrogant. Short, tortured small talk followed. I asked about housing options. As it turned out, they were all in the same dormitory. In any case, there was a lot of ice to break at this point.

Two hours later I stood helplessly in front of a large hospital with the inscription *All India Institute of Medical Sciences,* and unfortunately not in front of the dormitory, where in my mind I saw myself lying in a comfortable bed. The way here had already seemed much too long, and I still hadn't learned to point out my real destination to the rickshaw drivers exactly enough. In my hand I held the sweaty piece of paper where the writing was already illegible. Behind me on four lanes the traffic roared past. When the note was turned, the abbreviation of the dormitory looked like the letters AIIMS, which was undoubtedly the abbreviation of the large clinic I was now facing. My patience was slowly coming to an end. Just finding somewhere to stay, that was important now. Where, did not matter at all.

Again I shouldered my backpacks, which started to hurt my back, and walked across the campus. So I just had to get a room here. On the large lawns surrounding the tall 14-storey buildings, patients lay on mats. Mostly old people, some of them even had running infusions on their arms or hands, most of them were being cared for by relatives. The whole picture looked like after a big natural disaster or a train accident, where the victims were first taken care of outdoors until they were taken to hospital. After a few minutes of walking across the campus I arrived in front of a small side street, where some guesthouse signs were hanging on the walls.

I just took the first thing that came along. There were some bags of lentils and beans outside the door. The whole thing looked like a grocery store, which I liked very much. The room was supposed to cost the equivalent of two euros a night.

The first sight turned out to be a little strange, as it was actually not a real room. The walls did not reach up to the ceiling, so that it was rather a shed than a room. In a small niche there was a toilet bowl without a seat and a hose hanging out of the wall with a small water tap underneath. Nothing else. A small bucket, obviously for used toilet paper, was right next to the door. It was still half filled with brown cloths. I took the room and pressed a few rupees into the hand of the bearded landlord. After he closed the door, I took the bucket and threw it, without thinking about it, into the small light well next to the toilet. Loudly rumbling it fell.

I undressed, got my sleeping bag liner out of my backpack, hopped in and put my iPod in my ears.

Within seconds I was deeply asleep.

Düsseldorf central station, 08:32 pm

I'm sitting in a highway service station. There's only one lane. Countless cars laboriously manoeuvre past each other, drive jerkily fast and then get very slow again shortly afterwards. Nobody honks. It is very quiet. The cars rustle inconspicuously. I look outside through a kaleidoscopic window and see everything eight times, in changing geometric shapes. A car pulls up to the window and stops. It is completely covered with a brown fur on the outside. Four figures with blackberry-coloured capes get out and want to fetch me. They use a glass cutter to open the window between us. To escape I lie down flat on the floor. The carpet has many small projections whose coordinated movements take me lying down to an emergency exit. It tickles my neck. The four figures are still after me. The carpet gives me a little push and I can get up. The emergency exit opens by itself: I escape.

Alex

When I woke up, I felt like I had just fallen asleep. Still, or again, there was light. Next door there was excited shouting, two people were having a discussion. Then a loud rumbling in the corridor. I peeled myself out of the sweaty sleeping bag. My face felt puffy. I had not yet changed the clock, all sense of time was lost. Silently I stood on the bed and stretched to look over the partition. The next room looked more comfortable, mainly because there were posters on the walls and more luggage and private stuff scattered around. A man, who must have been about my age, walked back and forth excitedly. Around his belly he carried a belt pouch, which looked a bit ridiculous on him because of its stately size. The landlord stood in the doorway and gestured wildly. Obviously it was about the room. As I straightened up even further, the landlord suddenly looked up at me, stretched out his arm and suddenly pointed angrily at me too. I had no idea what was going on, but immediately there was a knock on my door and the landlord jumped in front of the bed I was still standing on and angrily started to throw the few belongings that I had unpacked so far into my backpack. Apparently I was to quickly clear the room.

Reluctantly I collected my things and stuffed everything quickly into my rucksack, then I got dressed, demonstratively put my things in front of the door and went into the next room. The door was half open, the landlord had meanwhile calmed down and watched every movement suspiciously.

My neighbor was still busy in throwing a considerable amount of little things that had apparently accumulated here over a long period of time into plastic bags. I knocked discreetly on the door. On a small table next to the bed lay *Steppenwolf* by Hermann Hesse.

"Hello."

My neighbour said only briefly and somewhat absently:

"Come in!" without even looking at me.

He was very tall and looked like he was working out regularly. With the knee-length shorts he wore a rather tight-fitting plum-coloured shirt with a big collar. You could clearly see he was angry, he was sweating and his temples were throbbing visibly. When I offered my help to pack up, he still hadn't really turned to me. Hectically stuffing a few books into a pillowcase, he said:

"You can take down the posters, we may need them later."

I now entered the room and started to take down the posters, mostly they were women's posters from the FHM-Magazine. Indian-looking ladies, with big breasts. But what impressed me the most: This guy had used the word *"we"* before there had even been a reasonable word exchange between us. While I was folding the posters together, I really wondered what *"we"* would need them for.

Because of the rather crude way my neighbour threw his belongings together and packed them in a makeshift way, the room was completely cleared out in almost five minutes.

I grabbed my backpacks and took some of my neighbour's bags and we dragged everything in front of the shop of the still grim-looking landlord.

The heat was unbearable again, and I got a little dizzy, so I dropped down onto my backpack and waited. My neighbor again started to argue with the landlord, but then broke off in the middle of it and sat down next to me. He fumbled a pack of cigarettes out of a bulging trouser pocket that had been placed on the side, put one in his mouth and offered me one too. We both sat there for quite a while and watched the hustle and bustle in the small dusty alley smoking. My cigarette was half smoked down and I was about to say something, just to say *something,* when he suddenly reached out his hand to me:

"Thank you. I am Alexander."

For the first time he looked at me directly and grinned. He had a really winning smile, his face was already very tanned and the skin on the bridge of his nose had started to peel.

Outdoor style.

"Moritz. No problem", I said just as briefly.

Strange situation. I had just been evicted from my rented shed in my underpants. My neighbour had been no different and now we were sitting here, smoking and hardly talking a word to each other as if it was the most normal thing in the world.

That's what I really liked. After a few minutes I already had this good feeling, which one could only have with a few people. To be silent next to each other without feeling the silence unpleasant. It was just okay like that. I was Moritz, he was Alexander, and we were both without an apartment in Delhi. Done.

Diagonally opposite, a boy crouched by the side of the road in front of an aluminium pot standing on a small petrol stove. I could see how he cut open individual small milk packets and poured them into the pot. Then he rummaged in his trouser pocket and threw in some brownish crumbs that he had previously beaten on a stone slab with the blunt side of a knife.

Aromatic fragrance.

When Alexander saw that I was watching the boy, he put out his cigarette and called out to him:

"Hey, Do Chai!"

Eagerly he immediately set about rinsing two small glasses in a bucket of water. Then he filled it with a ladle of brown milk tea and hurried over to us. Alexander gave him a few coins and handed me one of the two glasses. It smelled great of cardamom and other spices. Alexander toasted with me his and sipped the hot stuff. The first sip already made me really awake.

Masala Chai. What a great drink.

I drank *chai for the* first time when I was 13 years old. That was the name of the strange concoction they gave me to drink when I was with the boy scouts. My parents had enrolled me in the rangers when I was eight years old, and so I spent most weekends, but at least one day a week, in the forest and was allowed to learn all the animals off by heart. At some point I also had to take the so-called scout test. I had to name an enormous number of trees and plants, which was quite difficult despite weeks of practice.

The bigger boys had already started to cook black tea, wine, dried fruit and rum in a big pot at the campground in the afternoon. In the evening the scout test success was celebrated with large quantities of this mixture. After the third bowl I quickly became dizzy and nauseous. It tasted like warm muesli with brandy. I was one of the first in the tent, got diarrhoea and had to throw up several times. The next morning, with a hell of a headache, I was allowed to tell the younger rangers all about wetland maintenance and bat protection. One week later I became a forest godfather of my own godfather forest. My career climb as a ranger was steep. One week later I begged my parents to let me leave the forest youth.

"You can call me Alex."

Alex.

As a matter of course we started to think about where we could find accommodation. I learned that he had already moved several times, and from the nature of his report, that most of the time it could not have been done voluntarily. Somehow I had the feeling that it was better not to talk to him about it again for a while.

A few meters away there was another guesthouse where a few Europeans lived. Alex knew two Greek women there, a Frenchman and another German, from the big hospital next door. He was, like the others, a medical student in his final year and was doing an internship there. While we shouldered our luggage and slowly dived into the ever narrowing alley, I told him why I was here. He didn't make a face about it and just mumbled:

"Sounds good!"

The apartment was actually just a small room on the third floor with balcony and toilet. Yellowed wallpaper hung on the walls and the floor was covered with a layer of dirt several centimetres thick. Nevertheless, it was much better than the last room, and a lot of sunlight shone in. We rented the room for a few weeks and paid half in advance after the obligatory negotiation. Alex's first move was to push the two halves of the bed apart to the opposite walls. Then he climbed onto one of the beds and began to carefully hang the posters back up.

"You don't mind if I sleep out on the balcony, do you?"

"Nope."

"Very good, because I need a lot of oxygen."

We spent the rest of the morning cleaning the room. Alex got a bucket, a broom and a bottle of chlorine cleaner with which we almost poisoned ourselves. Around 3 pm it smelled like a swimming pool and the floor was shiny. Whatever had happened in this room before, our chlorine flush had successfully destroyed all traces of it. A small table, which Alex simply took from the staircase, completed our setup. The bathroom was pleasantly clean, we had a wardrobe and a balcony with two halfway decent chairs. I had quickly stowed my stuff away and went to sleep. Alex went somewhere.

Towards evening he came back and had bought a bag of ice and six bottles of beer.

Grinning, he poured the ice into the sink and put the beer bottles in. Then the door opened again and a slim young man came in.

A little sleepy, I sat up.

"This is Jacques."

Jaques was fully dressed in jeans. Everything in washed out look.

Eighties.

His eyes were bright and low set, which gave his face a brisk expression. Jaques came from Lyon, but had a German mother and therefore spoke German quite well, though with an unmistakable accent.

First he put a cigarette in his mouth and then shook my hand. You could feel how thin he was just by the way he shook his hand. I told him my name, and from that moment on he consistently called me Maurice. He did not even bother to pronounce the name in German. I was Maurice. He called Alexander Alec.

After he had inspected our room carefully, Jaques threw himself onto Alex's bed.

"You've made a nice nest, you two, ha, ha!"

He grinned widely and began to tell me about his day. Probably he thought I was a medical student too, because he seemed to assume that I had some prior knowledge of what he was talking about. Jacques had spent half the day in a small operating theatre, sterilizing Indian men under expert guidance. The Indian government had set up a program to establish some form of birth control in the overpopulated country. Every man older than 30 could get the snip for 1000 rupees or optionally a small transistor radio from Jaques to have his spermtubes cut without anaesthetic. Jacques hands performed the apparently very complicated operations in the air. Finally, he used his fingers to form scissors and cut two imaginary *vas deferens*. I had to shake myself.

"What can I say? The turnout is enormous. What do you think Maurice, do the boys, I mean, the boys who get cut in the sack without anaesthetic, do the boys most often want the cash or do they take the radio?"

"I think they'll take the money."

"Ha, hm, no, they take the radio, can you believe it, they take the transistor radio!" he said, slapping his thighs and leaving the room muttering.

Then he turned around and asked:

"How's the Ackermann action tonight?"

Alex looked at me. I shrugged my shoulders. Then he gave me the thumbs-up sign and closed the door.

"What is the Ackermann action?" I asked.

"Ackermann is an eccentric German-Indian who has been working here in surgery for years. He's got a kind of chief resident position there. He invited Jacques and me to a private barbecue tonight. You should definitely come."

"Really? But I don't know anything about medicine!"

"It doesn't matter!"

Duisburg central station, 08:45 pm

I am naked and standing in a fully tiled room. It looks like a kitchen, everything is completely white. As I get closer, I recognize individual boxes and cans on a worktop, all completely white. From the ceiling there is soft easy listening music, like in a department store. There is no exit anywhere. I turn around and stand in front of the fridge. When I open the door, the easy listening music changes to a loud Bossa Nova organ rhythm, and distantly there is also some noise of the sea. I can hardly see anything because there are bright rays of light coming out of the fridge and shining into my face. In the middle is a white box with the size of a cornflakes package. In black felt-tip pen writing it says: "Lemming-Crunch". The Bossa Nova beat forces me to eat a handful of it. It tastes like brittle.

Barbecue party

I've been in Delhi for 36 hours. I had founded a flat share, had a job in my pocket and an invitation to higher social circles for the evening. I guess you'd call that a run. Things were once again going better for me than expected.

While I was eagerly working on my lyrics on the notebook, Alex lay down on his bed and slept.

Dr. Ackermann must have been a colorful personality, from what Alex had told me. He lived in a villa in the embassy district of Delhi and was highly respected by the mostly foreign medical students. From an academic point of view, he was probably not held in such high regard. However, for reasons unknown, Dr. Ackermann, about 60 years old, had been a tolerated member of the surgical department for almost 20 years.

It was 7:00 and we had to go. I woke Alex up. He mumbled something, closed his eyes again and seemed to keep sleeping. I fished a lot of crumpled clothes out of my backpack.

Difficult. I wonder what was the best thing to wear on an occasion like this. It had to be something chic, in my opinion, at any rate.

Again I took a white shirt and long trousers, took a look in the mirror and was ready to go. In my trouser pocket I felt for a few notes, squatted on my bed and counted. Alex opened his eyes.

"Are you done yet?"

"Looks like it!"

He stood up jerkily, went to the front door and pulled himself up ten times quickly one after the other at the door frame. Then he began to rummage in his half of the wardrobe for a T-shirt. Alex told me that he had an incredible number of T-shirts. Wherever there were any shirts with stupid prints, he couldn't resist and bought it. Just like other people bought postcards or junk as souvenirs of visited countries and places, Alex invested in T-shirts. First he put on a red T-shirt with some socialist symbols printed on it, but with a smile he quickly took it off again, picked up the next one and asked me

"Say, this one or which one now?"

I pointed to a yellow T-shirt. He looked down contentedly at himself. It was a shirt with a comic drawing of Batman sitting in a beer bottle and in his underpants in an armchair. Next to Batman stood Robin with an unhappy face ironing his cape. I gave two thumbs up and grinned at Alex.

A note was hung on Jacques' door on the first floor. He had changed his mind at short notice and was on his way to another party with the two Greek women.

It was about half past six when we got into the motor rickshaw and chugged towards the city centre. Most of the time the driver in his khaki green rickshaw driver working suit was turning on his big sound system, which was tied together with bare wires. The Punjab music crackled considerably and just about drowned out the loud rattling of the engine. Above the moped handlebars there was a sticker: *Small Family - Happy Family!*

The journey took about half an hour. The air was stuffy, humid and dusty as usual. So sweat marks under the arms were quick to develop.

At the crossroads in front of the Gateway of India we turned off into the embassy quarter. The houses we passed gradually looked more and more colonial: Giant villas and townhouses behind high walls, with lots of green lawns in front of them. Brass signs showed most of the houses as embassies of smaller countries. Then the street was completely blocked with thick concrete cylinders. The driver stopped and pointed to a sign, a kind of signpost that showed the direction to the American embassy.

"You have to walk from here, only a few meters!" said the driver friendly.

The American embassy had been generously sealed off by roadblocks. But since Dr. Ackermann's villa was very close by, we had to get through somehow. Alex paid for the rickshaw, I went to a guard and asked for directions. After a long chat and some explanations we were allowed to pass the guard house and were accompanied into a side street by a heavily armed guard, who actually looked like a soldier in full battle gear.

We thanked each other well and ran, giggling into a driveway a little intimidated.

Dr. Ackermann' villa was well guarded. The walls were equipped with several video cameras.

It was a large house with colossal columns. In front of it there were about 30 to 40 guests standing around in small groups in the garden. It smelled of charcoal and barbecue. A middle-aged man, in a white shirt, stood in front of a gate. Alex went to him and gave his and Jacques' full names. Apparently we were on the list. We were let in immediately.

But nobody seemed to pay much attention to us. Dr. Ackermann was not to be seen. We went to a small table with a white tablecloth and took beer from a cool box with ice cubes. I looked around. There was only a motley crew of Indians and Germans out there, but nobody Alex knew from the clinic. Since we both had to pee urgently, we marched to the front of the building and tried to go inside. But in front of the big double-winged door stood a guard and shook his head mildly. At an open side entrance, catering staff walked in and out with trays full of barbecue skewers. Suddenly, Alex ran and dashed through the door, which slammed shut right in front of me. Inside, Alex was laughing. Then he opened the door a crack and let me in. It was nice and cool.

Smell of old wooden floor and cigarette smoke.

From the upper floor one could hear muffled music. We passed a pompous entrance hall with a bronze bust in the middle. Everything here seemed colonial. From the top of the large main staircase we heard a loud whooping. A sound that was supposed to sound feminine, but was certainly a man's voice. The atmosphere was eerie, Alex was beaming from ear to ear:

"Looks like we found the right party after all!"

Finally we found a toilet in the back corner of the hall.

I was washing my hands when suddenly someone behind me cleared his throat. Surprised, I turned around. A somewhat corpulent man in a too tight, light linen suit stood in front of me. The olive-green shirt was hanging out of his trousers, his already thinning hair stuck sweatily to his reddish-brown burnt neck. Then Alex came out of the cabin and also stopped silently.

Busted – I thought so.

Now they'd call security because we snuck into their private party. Still, nobody had said anything. Then Alex suddenly grinned broadly and shook the hand of the man in the linen suit cheerfully and effusively.

"Sommer, a pleasure. We haven't had a chance to introduce ourselves upstairs yet, but there's something happening today, isn't there?"

The man in the light suit looked at us alternately in astonishment. He seemed to be drunk and was thinking about how and where he should place us.

"A pleasure, Dr. Reisefleisch," he finally replied and then added in a wavering and somewhat lisping voice:

"But not a veterinarian, hahaha. Well, let's finish up here and get up to the bar."

On the stairs Dr. Reisefleisch became cautious again and asked shyly:

"But you're sure you're not interns? He specifically told me that those on the outside should have their own party and not be allowed inside!"

Alex placated our involuntary patron and told him some invented stuff. On the upper floor there were again two guards who looked at us suspiciously. Dr. Reisefleisch mumbled a code word and we were allowed to enter a hall where muted easy listening music was playing. 15 to 20 figures stood here in the candlelight of several upright chandeliers. The doctor went to a small minibar and conjured up three glasses. Enthusiastically he handled some bottles and mixed three reddish-brown drinks for us. He pressed a glass into my hand and told me in a confidential tone of voice:

"I mixed you a *Bohländer*!"

The drink tasted of mint, vodka and chocolate. Whatever Alex had told him must have inspired his complete confidence. Laughing, he also handed Alex a glass. I looked around. Most people, both men and women, avoided my gaze. They were all wearing surprisingly revealing clothes. The drink was good, the place was extraordinarily odd.

Numerous hunting trophies could be seen on the walls.

"And who is this?" I asked Alex.

A man in purple bloomers and a white naval officer's jacket stood in one of the back corners, surrounded by several figures devoutly listening to his words. Beneath the uniform jacket, a kind of leather corsage could be seen, which had not been tied all the way to the top, allowing a view of ample chest hair.

Alex leaned over:

"You mean the man with the clipped mustache? That's Dr. Ackerman."

Alex looked at me, I looked at the floor so as not to burst out in loud laughter. We both seemed to have internalized the uniqueness of this situation. Things you could only see once in a lifetime.

At the right place at the right time.

"Looks like you're in the right place at the right time!" said Dr. Reisefleisch.

Alex stammered and took a big sip from his glass. The doctor continued in a more intimate tone:

"Dr. Ackermann is a big fan of the leather scene. You know *Old Guard*, *New Guard*, that sort of thing."

"So Dr. Ackermann is gay?" Alex asked.

"I wouldn't necessarily say that. He's just very interested in homosexual culture, art and history."

At first it was hard to believe the doctor's words, especially when looking at the small crowd: almost everyone in the audience was dressed in skin-tight leather, black tight-fitting trousers with bulges in the crotch, leather vests or caps, and moustaches.

Dr. Reisefleisch meant for me and Alex to be quiet and follow him with a gesture. We went up to the small audience that had gathered around some small glass cabinets. When we came within earshot, Dr. Ackermann had just taken an object out of the display case that looked like an ice pick. He asked his listeners the question:

"Have you ever heard of Freeman's transorbital method?"

The listeners whispered in denial and Dr. Ackermann's gaze grazed me and Alex. For a short moment I had the feeling that Ackermann was frightened by the presence of us both but apparently Dr. Reisefleisch standing next to us vouched for us, so that he immediately continued to speak confidently. After a while Alex could unfortunately only keep himself on his feet and tried to lean on something with great difficulty.

While I was only worried that he didn't knock over any of the many exhibits in the room, the doctor looked at him with amusement. I also found it difficult to follow Ackermann's words, although they did not seem uninteresting.

The ice axe like object was passed on. Obviously it was a surgical instrument. I could hardly imagine for what kind of surgery such a martial instrument could be used, it was after all almost 50 cm long.

I was getting warm. For some reason my legs felt soft and the red carpet slowly started to make little waves under my feet. My heart was beating faster and scraps of words were coming to my ear:

"...a very inexpensive procedure... ...requiring little expertise... ...time constraints... short local anaesthesia... lasts only one hour..."

I turned around, Alex had fallen into an armchair behind me, his gaze seemed to be fixed.

It began to flicker again and again before my eyes. By squeezing my eyelids together I could repress the kaleidoscopic images of my surroundings, in between the voice of Ackermann, metallically booming:

"...tool inserted under the eye socket, along the top of the eyes... short blow, skull thinnest there... then advance to subjective assessment point."

The bystanders made moaning noises, Alex gurgled and whispered:

"Can you see that when you close your eyes?"

Dr. Reisefleisch was gone.

"...as I said, mostly just local anaesthesia, sometimes electric shocks... to question the patients... destruction of the grey matter perfect for impairment in arithmetic tasks, little blood... then the other side... As I said, only one hour gentlemen, no wounds, only two violet spots on the eyelids!"

Something was wrong, something went wrong, something had been put in mine and Alex's drink.

Heat.

Gasping.

Smile.

Probably that damn Dr. Reisefleisch. My muscles were totally relaxed. I was leaning against a display case, laboriously and sweating heavily. Alex gurgled louder and louder, at first nobody noticed, but when he started to grunt, the company turned around and for the first time really took notice of us.

"Alex!" I hissed.

"Shut up!"

Alex tried to sit up and screamed:

"And what's the ice pick for now?"

Suddenly there was absolute silence and somehow I realized that it would soon be time to leave the room, or better: the whole building, by the fastest route. I tried to move slowly and felt like I was stuck to the floor.

Palate numb.

The Dotor held the instrument in his hands, walked resolutely towards Alex, stopped half a metre in front of him and directed the apparatus towards his eye socket so that the pointed end almost touched his upper eyelid. Alex did not move and grinned uncomprehendingly. I was seized by panic. What a strange circus we had gotten ourselves into here. I glanced through the room and in my thoughts I walked the way to the double door through which we had come. Eight big steps should be enough, the problem would only be Alex. How could we be so intoxicated and full of narcotics? We could never move fast.

Dr. Ackermann took a breath and said:

"This was still used in the 19th century to operate homosexuality out of people's heads!"

Alex giggled, I couldn't wait any longer.

Without really intending it, I bumped into the display case I was leaning against. It fell over with a huge crash, but fortunately didn't break. Only under the greatest strain could I will to move my legs. I knocked the instrument out of Ackermann's hand, kicked Alex violently in the leg, grabbed his hand and dragged him out of the chair. The pain of kicking his leg must have woken him up a bit, because he held my hand tightly and I pulled him behind me like a mother who has to go shopping with a stubborn child. I counted the steps, it must have been at least eight, but strangely enough the door was still far away from us. I didn't dare to turn around, but Alex did. We were still standing with the others who were staring at us in disbelief, especially Dr. Ackermann in his bloomers. He scratched his chest and seemed a little perplexed. Alex shook the hand of one of the leather listeners and then suddenly he ran off and dragged me to the door. As if someone had selected the slowmotion and then pressed the play button, everything suddenly went very fast. Alex ripped open the door and we rushed down the marble stairs, accidentally pulling off one of the door handles and throwing it behind us, it rattled again. We were still running through the entrance hall, where I slipped briefly, outside hand in hand. The boring barbecue party was still going on, I grabbed a half-full six-pack of Kingfisher beer cans as I ran past, and we reached the street.

The barbecue visitors looked at us, Alex had saliva bubbles in front of his mouth and was panting like a dog. I had no idea how long we had been running, but nobody seemed to follow us. The embassy district was behind us and on a busy street I waved for a rickshaw.

We hopped in the back and I mumbled to the driver:

"Yusuf Sarai!"

Alex murmured:

"There are some things you need to explain to me. I didn't quite understand the whole evening..."

I gave him one of the canned beers. The driver heard the hissing as he opened it and bitched in Hindi. Alex gave him a pack of Beedi cigarettes, which he put in his pocket and from then on said nothing more.

Midnight.

I even cracked a beer myself and let the airstream and some exhaust fumes blow into my face. What the hell was going on in this town? This place was crawling with maniacs.

I don't know why, but we never talked about that night at Dr. Ackermann's again. Whatever was in those drinks made me sleep all Sunday.

The dean is a Brazilian hacienda owner. Nobody likes him. I decide to invade his property. To do so, I must use a trick to get past the guard anteater outside the main entrance. Silently, I scamper across a meadow in the semi-darkness. With every step I take there are muddy noises. My feet get wet and it smells of petroleum. I rush into the kitchen in completely filthy loafers and shout to the service personnel: "Bring me the shotgun, I'll hunt him down, I will!" The staff is delighted and whispers restrainedly. But someone gets me totally wrong and brings the dean out of his bedroom, down to the entrance hall. The dean pulls a handcart behind him, on which is strapped an old, bulky ECG device with a large monitor. Questioning looks in my direction. I talk my head out of the noose and explain that I am here exclusively to look at the antique ECG device. What a coward I am. Meanwhile, a really big party has developed at the house. People are dancing around each other. They're playing "Nights in White Satin." I have a big mustache and I'm smoothing it out. Then I give the dean a defiant look and leave.

Everyday life

My head was pretty sore on Monday morning. I'm sure it wouldn't have hurt so much if I could have slept another three hours. But I still had to report to the institute and show some good will. I imagined that with a little luck I would be back before one o'clock and ideally back in bed. Alex had already disappeared somewhere early in the morning, I had only heard the door for a moment. I looked at my wristwatch. It was already 7:45, at 8:30 Klaus Mordmüller wanted to see me at the institute. If I needed as long for the treck with the motor rickshaw as last time, then I was already much too late. With narrowed eyes I looked for some drinkable water. My mouth was dry as a fucking desert and I still had the nasty aftertaste of betel nuts in my mouth. I staggered into the bathroom and brushed my teeth dry, just with some toothpaste, quickly. There was still a strong smell of chlorine in here that made my eyes burn. I put on a fresh short-sleeved shirt, scraped some dirt from my lower trouser leg and took my shoulder bag with my notebook. In the hallway I met Jaques, he also looked quite puffy and grinned.

"Work sucks!"

I only held up my thumb in approval, then we walked silently together for a while through the alleys to the main street. At a kiosk I bought a small sealed bag of ice-cold yoghurt. The slightly sourish freshness did a lot of good. We quickly found a cheap rickshaw driver.

When I arrived at the institute, it was already a quarter past nine. The traffic had squeezed into the city centre like an endlessly long, stinking sausage, and it took me over an hour.

Rather excited I ran back to the first floor and searched the long corridor for the office I had already been in on Friday. The door to Klaus Mordmüller's antechamber was half open, nobody was there. Politely I knocked on the door frame, and when no answer came, I entered the room and went to the office door. Again, after knocking twice, there was no response. Carefully I opened a crack in the door. The room was empty. It was empty not only because Mr. Mordmüller was not sitting in it, but also because there were no chairs in it. The carpet was gone, the desk drawers were open, even the ugly posters had been removed from the walls. Where the posters had hung, the wood paneling had remained a little brighter. Perplexed and with an uncomfortable feeling in my stomach, I turned around. Someone passed by in the corridor. It was a woman, about mid-40, with a khaki-coloured costume, which was buttoned up to the neck. Her shoes were the same colour and had high heels. The whole thing was almost like a uniform.

A fantasy uniform.

I quickly jumped back into the hall.

"Excuse me..."

The lady turned around. Her face was covered with make-up.

"Do you know where Klaus Mordmüller is? I had an appointment with him!"

She looked at me critically. Then after some hesitation, she said:

"I'm afraid Mr. Mordmüller won't be able to be at your disposal. I'm afraid I have to tell you that whatever Mr. Mordmüller has arranged with you has lapsed."

"But he's the head of the institute."

"No, Mr. Mordmüller was never the head of this institute. I am!"

My gaze flitted very briefly at her name tag and then back to her face. She seemed to have noticed the short check nevertheless and pointed her mouth while talking. The name plate said

Rita Langhans.

"Mr. Mordmüller was just one of our editors, he was released from his work on Friday afternoon due to – let's say internal problems – and is on his way back to Germany. Now, if you'll excuse me."

Within a minute my plan had fallen through, and precisely because last weekend had left such a positive feeling in me, I fell all the more deeply now. *Damn it!*

The khaki woman was almost at the end of the hallway when I reached her:

"One moment, please!"

"Please, I' supposed start here today as a freelancer!"

I had quickly invented the *"free" in* addition

"I'm supposed to write articles for the online magazine, Mr. Mordmüller had all my references."

"Let's please not talk about Mordmüller anymore, an unpleasant thing."

She kept raising her eyebrows when she said the name. Then she looked at me again from top to bottom. It seemed to me as if she was trying to scan me in order to make a quick judgment about me as quickly as possible. Up close, she smelled strongly of *Venezia.* She had golden ear clips on her ears that were a bit too heavy and pulled her earlobes down a bit. She tried to radiate authority, which she succeeded in doing to a certain extent.

She hesitated.

"What's your name?"

"Moritz Kemper."

"Kemper, Kemper, your name sounds kind of familiar."

That was the moment to play my only wild card.

"You may know my father, Christian Kemper, who worked here years ago."

Her features brightened briefly.

"Oh, yeah."

A short film actually seemed to play through her memory.

"Freelancer for an online magazine, have you ever done this before?"

I lied to her, then I gave her one of my ready-made texts.

At the door of the institute I took a deep breath and looked at the clock: it was eleven. I could actually still manage to be back in bed before one. The headache had not got better because of the excitement.

I had barely saved my job.

Mrs. Langhans had sent me to the administration department, where I was to give my bank details and leave my telephone number. I didn't have an account in India, and after a lot of back and forth it was agreed that I could collect my money from administration every two weeks. I got 200 Euro per month. Not much, but enough for a good standard of living in Delhi. I did not want to save anything anyway. I would live from hand to mouth. That was enough for me.

The first days in Delhi flew by just like that. I slept in, looked for breakfast in one of the numerous snack kiosks on the main street in Yusuf Sarai and stopped by the institute about every other day to deliver one of my texts.

Alex usually got up before me, did his pull-ups at the door and sneaked out of the room. Most of the time he jerked at the door so loudly from outside that I woke up. I really had no idea why he did that. It sounded as if he wanted to make sure the door was closed, even though he knew I was still in the room.

This whole process had almost become a familiar thing. Until one morning when I woke up with terrible nausea.

The night before Alex, Jacques and I had gone to a new restaurant. Jacques had been so enthusiastic about the goat meat that I wanted to try it.

Now a brown, watery sauce was running out of my butt, without me being able to exercise any control over this bodily function. I just ran to the shaky toilet in our room. With unbelievable pressure I emptied litres of bloody-watery diarrhoea with relatively large, undigested goat pieces. I cursed every single piece of goat before I flushed it, but that was only the beginning. Alex just unlocked the door and did not take long to understand my precarious situation. Firstly, because the little stuffy room stank miserably, and secondly, because the toilet door never closed completely and you could watch each other pooping, so to speak. In the beginning, there was always someone who went to the small balcony out of decency but after a while we didn't care. So we got to know each other. Instead of standing at the door for a long time, Alex came to me and brought me water.

It took the spoiled old goat a total of four days to completely leave my intestine. No matter what I put in the top, it came out the bottom again within minutes. The toilet visits were announced by short cramps in my stomach. Then I knew that the clock was ticking, about ten seconds later the brown inferno broke loose. The distances between the toilet visits so short that I started to get naked and totally sweaty in the small bathroom. My notebook was by my feet, as well as several bottles of water and a piece of bread. At times I fell asleep with my head leaning against the wall from exhaustion. To vomit I only had to hang my head comfortably to the right in the sink. For the headaches I poured bags of salt, which I had taken from the plane, into my mouth. It worked surprisingly well. When nothing was pouring out of me, I watched movies on my laptop. That way I managed to spend a whole day in the toilet. My butt hurt a lot from sitting there all the time, but it was still better than shitting in your own bed.

An octagonal wooden mountain hut. Stuffed animals hang on the walls and line the shelves. Their eyes are made of glass and stare down at me. Lynxes, eagles and a marmot. The marmot watches me particularly closely. A door is not to be found. Everything is made of wood. The wood breathes all the air out of me. There's no knothole anywhere where fresh air can get through. I wear four Barbour jackets on top of each other and feel like a Babushka doll. I sweat a lot and look for a way out. Then the ceiling slowly sinks down. The marmot seem to be pulling up the corner of its mouth, while it sees how I can only stand bent over. The shelves collapse. I squat, lynx and marmot fall in front of me, they are dusty and smile at me brutally.

Rabies

I usually only visited the institute for a very short time, because I was being very careful not to meet the other interns. During one of my short visits I even noticed with one ear how they obviously talked disparagingly about me. But I couldn't care less about those idiots. I delivered good work and could always pick up my money on time.

On a somewhat cooler morning I delivered a text about Germany and the 1968 generation to the editor of the online magazine. As I was about to sneak outside, I met Rita Langhans, the boss, in the corridor. I knew that my further stay in Delhi was largely dependent on her goodwill, so I put on my brightest smile.

"You always make good contributions here, Kemper! The Holi festival is just around the corner, how about writing an article about it? Just compare the Indian festival with the German Carnival in the Rhineland! What do you think of that?"

I was a little bit offended, but reflexively played the happy one:

"Yes, that's a great idea, I'd love to!"

Some small talk followed, and then I quickly left before someone could impose more work on me.

If there was one thing I couldn't stand, it was carnival, and I was sure that I could hardly keep this aversion out of my text and would most likely ruin it. Anyway, it was a job and it meant that I could continue working.

I drove back to Yusuf Sarai and went to *Café Raj* where I had an appointment with Alex for breakfast. The small café was located right next to *Lohdi Park*, and from the terrace you had a fabulous view over the greenery, which was a welcome change in contrast to our usual dusty grey surroundings. The park was a popular meeting point for couples. Its numerous hedges and corners offered an ideal and discreet meeting point for any intimacy between people in the otherwise very conservative society.

Alex was already sitting on the wooden terrace sipping from a large cup of chai tea. Into a padded wicker chair I let myself fall next to him.

We both ordered fried eggs, toast and coffee. I had another pineapple juice. Although it had rained briefly in the night and the lawn was still wet, there were already numerous visitors in the park. While I was hungry and drank the juice all at once, Alex searched the park with narrowed eyes until he finally, like a hunter who had found his prey, gave me a hand signal and hissed softly:

"There's two again!"

I looked in his direction, and there actually sat a young man in a light shirt, leaning against a tree and next to him a woman in a dark blue sari. She had put her scarf over his lap, and even at that distance you could clearly see her hand disappearing under the scarf and moving up and down. It was a strange spectacle in the early morning. The mere fact of watching two people having sex in public at breakfast was disturbing. What's more, Alex was obviously turned on by the fact that he was watching them. Heaven knows how many times he had come here before. Alex's thoughts were dirtier than a drug dealer's hands. In the end, I didn't care either. This country was crazy anyway. So Alex fit in perfectly.

But Lohdi Park was also an ideal place for jogging. In the past I had run a lot and it had always given me the feeling of being in control. I had not jogged for years now. Maybe it was Delhi with its unholy daily chaos, or maybe it was my own aimless way of life, in any case I decided to go running again in the evening. That way I could clear my head and bring my thoughts in order. But probably I would want to lie in bed in the evening and have the feeling that I had done something useful during the day.

The first time I ventured out in the evening to run to Lohdi Park, I realized after only 20 meters that it hadn't necessarily been the best idea to take many deep breaths in a city of millions with exhaust fumes and smog. Panting I stopped after another 100 meters and leaned on my knees. I felt like an old man. My heart was racing, the smoking and frequent drinking had left its traces without a doubt. The sweat ran down my legs and dripped onto the ground. I could just as well have gone running in the afternoon, because subjectively there was no difference in temperature. It just didn't get any cooler in this city.

I had bought cheap, used and already very sweaty Nike sneakers at a market. But with a little detergent from the tube they looked like new again and looked quite good on me, I thought. Despite all the adverse signs my body tried to send into my consciousness, I slowly walked on and finally found my rhythm.

Starry Starry Night.

The green lung of the Lodhi Park did the rest, and so I was soon able to run the first laps without interruption. I started to sleep better at night, I felt pain in my calves and thighs when I got up and enjoyed the growing feeling of getting closer to my old fitness again. When I got home, Alex had usually already fetched a bag of ice and was waiting for me with cold Kingfisher beer. He was already sitting on the balcony, I sat silently next to him, drank the beer and felt great.

It was one of those evenings that we finished on the balcony again, when Alex suddenly jumped up and wanted to go out. Since he noticed that I was rather less inclined to get into a crowd of people at a late hour, he began to create dazzling pictures of the two of us in bars.

Full of verve, he spoke of a little drink after work and then *drifting* home. *sullied by the luck of the night.*

He quickly talked me into it. We took a taxi to Connaught Place.

On the way home, I was bitten by a dog.

Alex and I were a little drunk and walked through the small streets of Yusuf Sarai.

Hey Kid RocknRoll, nobody tells you where to go.

Probably, without knowing it, I had invaded the dog's territory or scared him. He came silently, without barking beforehand, out of a niche and bit his way briefly into my forearm. I was very startled and shook my arm. The dog, who was not even that big, let go of me immediately and growled sinisterly while we ran away.

The shirt had some bite holes, and a warm sticky feeling spread to the palm of my hand. Vibrating nerves, endorphins. I was bleeding, dripping. When we had run far enough, Alex pulled me to him and lit his gasoline lighter to examine the wound. It wasn't until I saw the bite marks that it hurt. Alex took a deep breath, then lit a cigarette from the lighter, greedily sucked in the smoke and let it snap shut.

"Have you been vaccinated against rabies?"

Hell Yeah. No.

I wasn't sure. Alex pulled my arm and explained that we would have to traipse to the emergency room now. I would need some injections and the wound would have to be cleaned. I was a bit annoyed, especially when Alex started to tell me everything he knew about rabies:

"This is a very strange infection. First you are terribly thirsty, then you are disgusted by water, get gullet cramps and hallucinations. And then you're dead." *Great.* Still, I was glad he was there just now.

The emergency room of the AIIMS at three o'clock in the morning was not a place where people liked to go voluntarily. Outside the door was an immensely long queue of waiting people who, on closer inspection, all had some minor or major bleeding wounds and were kept outside by the guards, sometimes in a very rough tone. Alex showed them his AIIMS pass and they let us in immediately.

Inside there was even more chaos. This is how I imagined the field hospitals in World War I. It was stuffy, there were wounded lying everywhere, some of them unconscious, but most of them screaming miserably on couches or on blankets on the floors of the corridors. Alex explained that this was a normal situation, in a normal night. On tiptoe he led me through the many seriously injured on the floor into a room where accident victims were being sewn together on three couches at the same time. Most of them weren't moving anymore. Alex said laconically:

"They're patched up briefly here, and if they're still alive, they'll go into surgery eventually. Do you have any rupees left?"

I still had a grand in my pocket and some small dusty bills. Alex took it all and said he'd be right back. I sat down on a chair in the corner. A man of about the same age lay on a couch in front of me and opened his eyes occasionally. We looked at each other. The bandage on his temple continued to soak with blood, little by little.

The three nurses, who alone were in charge of the sewing room, were taking care of another patient who had run in front of a bus, drunk. When the guy started to fight, I saw how the stronger of the two slapped the injured man with full force and shouted at him in Hindi. After that he held still and stayed lying down.

My wound had stopped bleeding by now. Next to me stood a small metal container with gauze bandages,

I took two out and wrapped them around my arm. The man on the platform in front of me opened his eyelids again and looked at me. Then he moved his lips and formed words that I could not understand. He sighed slightly and closed his eyes again. I took a handful of gauze bandages, stood up and pressed them on the bandage on his head that was bleeding through. I could see that the blood had already formed a small puddle behind his head.

A short time later Alex came back with a small paper bag in his hand. He took a look at the man in front of me and murmured softly and a little annoyed:

"He's not breathing, can't you see? Why are you getting so close to his blood with your wound?"

My stomach contracted.

A soft, high-frequency sound in my ears.

The air suddenly felt even heavier. I saw the room in front of me getting longer as if in a slow backwards zoom.

Rotational fraud.

Alex's big hands pushed me back into the chair.

"Sit down over there."

Alex grabbed a few ampoules from the paper bag, sutures and individually wrapped bandages, then walked across the dirty floor into a corner and used pliers to get instruments from a tub of liquid. I saw that it had a rust-red colour when it was drained.

Alex washed the instruments and put them briefly into a machine that looked like it was from the Second

World War. The thing was steaming sideways and hissing. And I'm left to believe that everything was sterile now.

While the nurses told each other funny stories, laughing loudly, Alex started to clean the bite wound and sewed a bigger tear together. Before that he had anaesthetized my arm locally, so I only felt a slight pinch. I was impressed by the dexterity with which Alex tied knots despite the many drinks, and how skilfully he guided the small curved needle.

Advantage Moritz.

The sweat ran down my back and dripped onto the floor. Probably to distract me, Alex told me the strange story of a pathologist who, after Albert Einstein's death, secretly removed his brain against his last will and carried it around in a jar for years.

"The guy was caught by a private detective years later and didn't return the brain until then!"

"Medical humor," I pointed out.

"Nah, the truth!"

After I got a bandage, I had to get up and get some injections. Two against rabies, and two against tetanus, the last injection stabbed Alex in my right thigh.

When the needle with the syringe was stuck in my leg, I had to sit down, even more sweat ran down my back.

I'm about eight years old. In my grandparents' garden I'm playing under the old walnut tree in summer.

The dartboard I have placed at head height. I was about to turn around when something jumped at me and bit my leg. My thigh hurts and my mate Hendrik from the neighbourhood is muttering "sorry" as he runs away. The dart bounces up and down while running. I imagine my whole trousers already soaked in blood sticking to me. My father pulls out the dart and sprays something cold over it. Not even a drop of blood comes out of my leg.

"So, let's get out of here. We'll do your dressing changes tomorrow at our place! You can remove the stitches yourself after ten days.

I was sitting there pretty slumped and still staring at the bunk opposite. I had hardly said a word the whole time.

Big carnival of emotions.

"Come on!"

When we went outside, I saw Alex greeting some doctors. I felt dazed and noticed them smiling at us. Some of them stood around a cot and performed CPR. One of the doctors, a very young looking one, briefly interrupted the chest compressions to raise his hand in greeting.

"This is Balu."

Alex said to me and returned his greeting.

"He's only been here a couple of weeks either."

The young man did indeed look even fresher.

Alex made a very relaxed impression on me regarding his work in this hospital. He was always a little late, sometimes he just took a day off. I remember that his Indian colleagues always looked at him with astonishment. Only later did I read somewhere that every year about 75,000 people applied for a place at AIIMS, but only 0.06% of them were admitted per year. Those who worked and studied here were inevitably members of an elite. Alex seemed to disturb the place considerably with his certain, but mostly semi-serious manner and his ability to laugh at himself constantly. I think that's why he impressed most Indian colleagues, no matter where he appeared.

Dortmund station, 09:21pm

I drank four cups of coffee and quickly got a tremendous stich in my side. I'm here way too early. In the café I have to pay with potato crisps. Two medium sized crisps for each cup. The waitress is a bit corpulent. She goes from table to table on roller skates. Her name tag says Marcy. I count eight potato chips from my purse bag on to the table. With her flat hand, Marcy beats the stack into small crumbs. Then she pushes the greasy crumbs together on the table with one hand and throws them into her mouth with the other hand. She smiles slightly and keeps eye contact with me.

Oh, I say.

Marcy rolls behind the counter and I take my trench coat, my brown hat and go outside. At the hospital across the street I take a seat in the waiting room. On the door it says J.P. cardiac masseur. A receptionist asks me to come in. I take off my shirt. The receptionist takes it in silence and hangs it in a metal locker. With a felt-tip pen she writes my first name on a small wooden board. She puts it on the floor and pushes it over to me with a jerky foot movement. I take the sign and am led into a room without windows. A man in an undershirt stands here and looks into a corner. When I come in, he turns around. He has a nice mustache. Around his neck he has his name in gold letters on a gold chain: Jean Paul. He nods at me and I lie down on the floor on a mattress with a brown corduroy cover.

It takes ten minutes to massage my heart. Jean Paul then takes the wooden board with my name on it and hits it with a nail and a hammer against the wall next to numerous other boards. I put my shirt back on and leave. When I go out I feel much better.

Abysses

Every time we left our apartment, Alex turned around again after five meters and checked by jerking the door handle whether he had really locked the room door twice. The lock was so ramshackle and rickety that surely only a single kick would have been enough to open the door. But when I called out to Alex during his inspection:

"Leave it alone, anyone can get this thing open anyway," he turned jerkily and shouted loudly in my face:

"Now I have to start all over again!"

I was totally scared and preferred to keep my mouth shut. In silence we went to dinner.

When we sat on our balcony in the evening drinking beer, I spoke to him about his outburst of rage. I suspected the whole time that something about Alex's behavior must have its deeper reasons. He fumbled a cigarette out of the packet and went to our apartment. I heard the sound of the gas lighter and smelled the smell of a freshly lit cigarette. He inhaled heavily, blew out the air just as audibly, and stepped out onto the balcony again. At first I thought he didn't understand my question, then suddenly he started talking in a low tone.

"You like horror stories?"

"Yes, I do!" I lied.

I hated horror stories.

"Well, I didn't mean any harm when I yelled at you."

His voice now sounded almost subdued, and I was even ashamed to have even addressed the subject.

"Remember what you did in the summer of 1995?"

I thought for a moment.

"I think I was in Spain with my parents for the summer holidays."

Alex sat down and angrily pulled his cigarette. Then he clapped his flat hand on his thighs.

"Everyone was on holiday in the summer of '95, my parents and sister were also on holiday in Spain. Only I was allowed to stay in Germany, because my parents thought it would be better for me to be treated properly."

Alex started to tell everything about his summer '95 in a calmer voice. He told of his first visits to the child and youth psychiatrist after he had spent eight hours in the kitchen at home, standing in one spot to check the stove. His parents had found him sweating and shivering when they came home from work in the afternoon. He had not been able to go to school in the morning because his parents had left the house before him that day. During his usual inspection tour he had simply stuck to the stove.

Before that, he had always managed to hide the compulsion to control everything around him from his family. But on this day he had not been able to find a way out of the vicious circle of controls as usual, and his parents complained *that the boy was not normal.*

Alex told me that his parents did not understand his behaviour and could not or would not help him out of the confused world of his compulsions. He was watched daily: his checking of windows, clocks and taps before going to bed, and getting up at night to repeat the entire round of checks. His parents were aware of everything and decided to send Alex to an institution for the summer holidays. So they hoped to have a normal son back after their vacation.

"I spent six weeks in a room with a fat nine-year-old boy. What a stupid idea to hook up with him.

"Why?" was the first thing I said after a long silence.

"Because the little punk had the urge to count. They probably thought that it was best to bunker the compulsive ones all together! So I helped myself.

"How?" I asked.

"This summer, between the many therapy sessions, therapeutic painting and crafting and all the other nonsense, I started reading vampire books. There was a big library in the adult wing. I used to sneak in and take the books into my room. Among the vampire books, there was one about werewolves fighting vampires. It was a stupid story in itself, but when I read the first few lines about werewolves, things changed for me."

Now he talked more excitedly again and lit another cigarette on the old one.

"You know what they call the werewolf in the Rhineland?"

I shook my head.

He told me that the werewolf in the Rhineland is called *Stüpp*. Alex had grown up near Cologne. In contrast to the many legends and stories about blood-thirsty man-ravaged werewolves, people there were frightened of the *Stüpp* for another reason.

Alex now used his hands more and more when telling the story and accompanied every sentence with gestures. He revealed to me that he had found out in the library of the institution that the *Stüpp* was lying in wait for the full moon and jumped on a person from behind from a dark corner to hold on to his back.

Alex made a claw hand in my face.

He acted just as weird as most of the things he told me, but I knew he was more serious about this. I didn't make a face and just nodded my head.

"The special thing is that once it has ambushed you and is sitting on your back, it gets heavier with every step you take. There are few chances to get rid of him, because with every attempt to shake him off, he gets heavier. "You carry the son of a bitch around with you until you're insane with fear and finally collapse under his weight..." "And then", Alex took another short break, pulled greedily on his cigarette and said, while the smoke came out of his mouth and nose:

"Then you are dead..."

He looked up at the sky.

Alex explained to me how he decided this summer, without the help of the doctors, just with his own ideas and thought techniques, to simply stop being afraid and throw his *Stüpp* off his back.

"One must not show fear of compulsion from the very first moment. You understand, man, I've been self-treating!"

He tapped his fist on his skull and took a big sip of beer.

"I still have a few problems now and then, but all this old shit won't come back! I shook off my werewolf! There are people out there who carry their personal shit around with them all their lives because they're scared of it and run away. I ain't running from shit no more!"

"I'm the fucking Werewolf Killer! "

In the following days Alex often looked at me slyly when he checked our door lock. I laughed most of the time, and when I made a judo move, like throwing an opponent off my back, Alex laughed too.

The first weeks flew by just like that and I could really say that I felt very comfortable in Alex's company. But Jacques and the Greek girls were also nice. In the evenings we went out for dinner together, later on we mostly sat on the roof, drank beer and watched the colourful hustle and bustle on the street.

All in all it was the most pleasant weeks in Yusuf Sarai. Only two things bothered me:

Firstly, that so often in the institute when I was delivering my texts I clashed with the snooty young staff, they apparently thought I was enormous competitian in the job and could not cope with my casual way of working.

Second: Nick Limburger, a medical student from Germany who lived in the room above us. A polytox-icomaniac and eccentric who made no secret of the fact that he found it incredibly cool to be a fully trained doctor soon. Nick drank without a break, and when he was already terribly drunk in the early evening, he would scream to himself. Sometimes he threw one of his plastic chairs from the balcony and swore about all the *"Indian assholes"*. I think the landlords were afraid of him. Occasionally he would stand outside our door and knock on it for hours, completely drunk. He looked pitiful in his worn Adidas clothes, his sunburned face and the crazy look. At a flea market he had bought a North Korean army jacket, which he often put on and then marched up and down the corridor doing a goose step. I was always very happy when he was gone.

I remember one night when he barged back in. His face was sore and bloody, his right cheek a single graze. Nick had put some makeshift toilet paper dressing on it. His clothes looked just as tattered. He proudly told us about his weekend trip to Goa and the "hip full-moon parties" that were celebrated there every day, full moon or not. He had got pills from some people and danced the whole night through. At dawn he had not found the way back to his bungalow and had fallen down a three meter high cliff. Down below he had fallen on a coral-lined rock and was only woken up by beach walkers after a while. For Nick this was *the* sensational story. Maybe he wanted to prove something to me with this or needed attention. I don't know.

One night Alex said completely out of context:

"Moritz, I think this Nick is half wolf and half human: one side wants to fuck, drink and destroy, the other wants to think, read and laugh..."

As disturbing as this statement was, it probably still applied to most of us.

I thought a lot about friendship that same night. The friendship that Alex had shown me every day gave me a feeling that I hadn't felt for a long time, especially because of his openness. Memories that I had repressed somewhat successfully in recent years suddenly came back. Washed out and blurred in the places I had tried to forget, but painfully detailed in the moments I did not want to lose.

I remembered this warm summer night, the window in my children's room was half open, on me was only a thin summer blanket, but I was still sweating. The air pressed everything down harder and harder, and it was only a matter of a few minutes before the longed-for thunderstorm finally brought the cooling I had hoped for. My room was in third floor, and so in summer most of the heat always piled up in my little four walls. Nevertheless, I preferred it that way, because here I had peace. With the thought that I would probably be able to sleep much better when the rain finally started, I sat up and grabbed my glasses. The small illuminated numbers of my alarm clock told the time: shortly after midnight. Tomorrow I had to go to school again. The weekend had passed much too quickly. Soon there would be school reports and summer holi-

days. But what interested me most was whether Hendrik couldn't sleep because of the thunderstorm either, so I got up, went to my desk and looked out of my gable window through the curtains.

Hendrik was my best friend. He was 13 years old like me and we had known each other since kindergarten. We spent every spare minute together, made the same model kits together, had sat next to each other in school since the first grade and had secrets with each other whose deeper meaning could only be understood as thirteen-year-olds.

Two years ago, to my greatest joy, he had also moved to my immediate neighbourhood. His parents had moved into the house opposite the small village market place. An old half-timbered house with steep stairs inside and very cosy. Our house was diagonally opposite, only 100 meters away, and only two weeks ago we had started using flashlights to signal to each other at night to make an appointment for a walkie-talkie conversation. The only problem was that his room was not as well sealed off as mine, but on the middle floor, and right next to his parents' bedroom. So we had to watch out like hell, because Hendrik's parents were strict. Hendrik had already been warned twice by his father to be quiet at night. For a week he had taken away his walkie-talkie as punishment. In spite of everything Hendrik could answer me silently with the torch, even when he was awake. I was groping for my torch in the dark room, which I normally always put next to the bed, when suddenly the first flash of lightning lit up my little room. The cold flash of light that briefly illuminated everything as bright as day was enough to find the flashlight. My father had brought me the torch from the hardware store, it needed three thick batteries, the biggest of all, and unfortunately the power consumption was immense. But it shone a distance of 150 meters and could conjure up a real cone of light in the night sky. From my pocket money I could never afford the high battery consumption, but in a miraculous way there was occasionally a new pack on my staircase. Unlike Hendrik's parents, my father knew all about our nocturnal Morse and radio conferences. He didn't talk to me about it, but he let me feel that he took good notice of it, if not even had some pleasure in it.

I did not need to count for long, because the thunder followed the lightning breathtakingly fast. The thunderstorm was now right above our village, and the first small drops announced the impending storm. First the rain ticked only softly on the roof, then the intensity increased rapidly and became a mighty hissing.

I pushed the curtains all the way to the side and was able to see the whole market place, all the way over to Hendrik's house. The fact that our house was also located directly at the market place had always given me a feeling of security. A small fountain with movable bronze figures marked the middle of the oval square, and the old houses surrounded it so that the shape resembled a semicircle.

Third window from the left, that was Hendrik's room, but there was no light on. While it was flashing again, and the rain was pattering loudly down on the dry cobblestones, which were still warm from the day, I sent my big beam of light into Hendrik's window and flashed twice. Hendrik's room was much bigger than mine, but his bed was just under the window in such a way that my beam of light had to fall exactly on the wall of the headboard of his bed. Only about 50 centimetres above his pillow.

Still nothing moved. The air finally began to get pleasantly cool, the market place was literally steaming, and a wonderful smell of freshly sprinkled earth rose up to me.

In none of the adjoining houses was the light on. Everything seemed to be extinct and the longer I imagined to be the only one experiencing this thunderstorm spectacle, the more eerie it became. Hendrik apparently slept too soundly. I hoped that he had at least left the walkie talkie on. I did not want to experience the storm without him. Besides, I knew that I would fall asleep much better if I could at least have talked to him briefly beforehand and moan about the end of the weekend. I grabbed the walkie talkie and leaned out of the window a bit, the antenna had to stick out as far as possible, otherwise the reception was too bad.

Just for a short moment I looked down and that's when I saw the shadow for the first time. Only for a second I had saw that a dark shadow stood in front of the door of the neighbouring house. Scared to death and with an exorbitant heartbeat I immediately flinched back into the window.

My heart would not stop racing, I did not know what to do first. I put the walkie talkie on my desk, the lamp I held tightly with my other hand. If only Hendrik would at least wake up. What had I just seen there?

Long after midnight, in the middle of a violent summer storm? Although I would have much rather gone to bed and wanted to pull the blanket far over my head and shoulders, I gathered all my courage and carefully approached the window again. Then I leaned forward slightly and looked down again. There was no doubt about it, and the moment I realized that the shadow down by the neighboring house, only about nine meters away from me, was a figure with a black hood, I began to hear my own heart beating loudly in my head. Then the pounding turned into a stupefying murmur. And the certainty that someone was standing outside the door or window down there, in the middle of the pouring rain, made a cold shiver run down my back. In Hendrick's room there was still no light. Just when one needed it most.

I didn't know what to expect from this situation. It felt hopeless. Our neighbors weren't home, it went through my mind. What could I do? Here in my father's house, I felt safe. So I grabbed the flashlight and was just about to point it when I felt the screw cap on the battery compartment, which seemed to be not quite tight, come loose and fall down as if in slow motion and before I could lean out any further to catch it.

I was in a dither. While hundreds of thought fragments crumpled up in my head, the lid of the flashlight bounced off the pavement just behind the dark figure. The figure remained motionless, and at the same moment, when a flash of lightning illuminated the night sky, I saw the dark figure orienting itself upwards along the front of the house until, under the dark hood, I blurred in the rain, for a split second, believing I saw a completely white face.

I thought my heart would stop in the next moment and threw myself backwards into my room, with all my might where I hit my back hard on the floorboards. How dazed I lay there, first my back was tingling, then it soon began to hurt. But the certainty that my spontaneous, thoughtless action had led to the shady figure drawing even more attention to me, stunned me again.

There was no light coming from Hendrik's room. The rain slowly subsided, and when I had calmed down a bit, I stalked timidly to the window again. The shadow at the bottom of the house had disappeared, the market place was bathed in the same peace and darkness as before.

I waited in vain the rest of the night for light from Hendrik's room.

Something had changed.

Hendrik was dead and a flashlight signal never came from him again. I experienced the turn of the school year without him, and in autumn my parents moved with me to Hamburg for professional reasons. Hendrik had not said anything to anyone. I had been thinking about it for months and actually I still think about it today with the same perplexity. Where had the signs been, where was the moment when you could have stopped everything? Hendrik's sister had once told me that she was convinced that it must have been her fault. She confided in me that she had not kept her skipping rope in her wardrobe that evening, as usual, but had left it on the corridor in front of Hendrik's room.

I was now 14 years older than Hendrik, although we had once been the same age and had shared everything with each other for a while. And if someone asked me what true friendship felt like, then I would tell them about everything I had been allowed to experience with Hendrik, until that one night, when I saw the shadow in front of our house.

Münster central station, 09:57 pm

I'm lying in a beautiful, spring-like flower meadow. A mountain world with snow-covered peaks surrounds me. I don't know how I got here. When I reach into my pockets, I feel oatmeal. In front of me the mountain meadow falls away steeply. I lie on my back and look at the sky. The clouds slowly condense into an opaque blanket. The sun shines stronger and stronger, so that a dark-yellowish light is created. Suddenly I hear a loud noise of propeller engines. At the last moment I roll to the right, and there the fuselage of a 4-seater Twin Otter propeller plane crashes into the meadow next to me. The wings are torn off, and in the cargo hold there are 20 protective helmets in neon colours. I take a yellow helmet and try it on. It fits perfectly.

Festival of colours

On Some days I had no idea what day of the week it was. Time went by very fast, and mostly one day resembled the other. I never got bored. When Alex came out of the hospital in the early afternoon, we usually jumped into a taxi and explored Delhi to the last corner.

"Every culture has its intoxicants. In Africa they chew cat, in South America they chew coca, in Europe they smoke and in Asia they chew betel nuts. Chewing weird stuff until you get dizzy has been part of the culture for centuries."

Alex's remarks were of captivating clarity. One evening, he showed me where the best betel nuts were available in Yusuf Sarai.

At the small stand a small old woman sat behind a very high counter. On the sales area in front of her there were all kinds of small bowls with powders and extracts. We were in an evening mood, put two ten-rupee notes on the counter and ordered two portions of betel. The old lady grabbed a green leaf and, with her pointed fingers, quickly gathered some ingredients and put them in. I couldn't identify all the ingredients: a sticky paste that smelled of liquorice, chopped unripe betel nuts, powder that looked like spices, and finally from a tube, on the outside like from a hardware store, probably some slaked lime. Then she folded the leaves into two elaborate little packages and handed them to us. We put them in our cheek pouches. Alex looked like a hamster.

I took two hearty bites of the leaves and the bitter-sweet juice of the betel nuts rose against my cheek mucosa. Alex looked at me. We could not speak, blood-red drops were already coming out of the corners of his mouth.

The euphoric effect came fast.

Giggling and slightly swaying we took the way through the back alleys, past the many craftsmen and workshops and spat out red crumbs in front of us alternating.

We were smiled at.

The people in our little corner were as if they had changed over the following days. Days before the actual Holi festival, the narrow paths were filled with hustle and bustle. From our balcony I could see how small fires were lit in front of the doors and in the backyards. Little straw figures were thrown into them.

The glow of fire in the many small alleys gave the evenings something mystical.

I had prepared myself conscientiously for my research on the Holi article and scoured a few internet sites. As with most Indian festivals, tomorrow the triumph of good over evil was celebrated. When I thought of the pictures from the Cologne Carnival or Weiberfastnacht on the Cologne Cathedral Square, I involuntarily had to remember that in Germany it certainly had to be the other way round during carnival. Holi was the festival of colours. Everyone, no matter what caste they belonged to, would be in each other's arms tomorrow with their neighbours and then throw or smear themselves with colour powder. I was really curious. Days before the big newspapers had started to criticize the Holi holidays for their otherwise rather unusual high consumption of alcohol. So the week promised to be interesting. The good thing, of course, was that the festival lasted three days in the middle of the week, and I had already signed off on Monday under the pretext of research at the institute until the following week. My article was not to appear until the next issue of the online magazine.

In the morning we woke up quite early by loud screaming on the street.

I had only just managed to slowly straighten up and squat on the edge of the bed to look over to Alex from puffy eyes when there was already a heavy knock at the door. It couldn't have been Nick, he mostly just kicked at it. It was Jaques, whose French accent sounded excitedly through to us.

"Wake up! You gotta see this!"

I got up and opened the door. Jacques stood outside the door with the Greek girls and stormed straight into the room. Alex turned around with a mutter. A couple of gruff pokes woke him up for good. Half asleep we only put on our slippers and followed the others up the stairs to the roof terrace. From here we had a perfect view over the whole district. Jaques pointed his finger in the direction of the main street and then hit his thighs. The whole street was full of people, adults and children throwing water bombs at each other, wetting each other with spray guns or just hugging and sprinkling them with paint powder or coloured water. I had expected a lot, but this sight left me and all present speechless. The bright colours were visible for more than 100 metres up to us, the city seemed to have turned into one single wild coloured mob.

Ten minutes later we were in the middle of it.

I was hit particularly hard right at the beginning. As soon as I set foot in the alley. A water bomb landed vertically on my head from an upper floor full of grinning children. While the others sensed the ambush, I was already standing in the middle of the alley and was defenceless against further water bombs. I was able to avoid two thick charges, one hit me in the back. Alex and Jaques laughed and lit beedi cigarettes. Then we ran to the main road.

It smelled of food, and during the night numerous stalls had been set up. At every corner one got small pigment bags and spray guns. After a short time Alex was hugged by so many people that his face shimmered in green, pink and blue.

My stomach was growling, and when I went to a stand to buy a small portion of somosas, a young man jumped at me from behind and poured a complete bag of pink colored powder over my head. I had to cough immediately and had the bitter chemical taste of the powder on my tongue. The smiling face I looked into afterwards was that of Balu from the emergency room.

He hugged me so warmly and wished me *Happy Holi* that I could hardly be angry with him. Then Balu held a bottle out to me.

Pure rum.

Thankfully I took a strong sip, but only briefly rinsed my mouth with it and quickly spat the stuff out again in an unobserved moment. Two other friends of Balu giggled and started to knead the pink powder neatly into my hair with their fingers. I quickly sensed that any resistance that day would be futile and gave myself over to the prank. The small group of doctors greeted the three just as effusively, with Alex and Jaques often having to stand protectively before the Greek women. One or the other tried to touch the two ladies while congratulating them.

From Balu we learned that a big buffet was set up at the deanery building at noon. We arranged to meet there.

Around eleven Jaques and Alex were beyond recognition smeared with colours, only the Greek women still had unblemished skin. Jaques and Alex had fortified themselves with rum and pushed their way through the crowds. In a small side alley I stopped to buy a cup of goat yoghurt. The dealer had painted a colourful sign with the inscription "*Bhang*". The clientele was queuing up.

The yoghurt cost only five rupees and tasted very spicy. The resinous consistency of the hashish pollen, which was processed into *bhang* here in combination with liquorice and other spices, gave the yoghurt a distinguished flavour. The Greek women also stood next to me spooning. When I had finished my meal, we looked at each other and I said, rather out of embarrassment:

"Hmm, yummy," and stroked my stomach in the process.

Out of embarrassment, I grabbed another yoghurt cup and started spooning. Alex came back with Jacques from another alley. The two of them had bought some more paint, because Jaques had thought about the constant harassment of the Greek women and had come to the conclusion that they looked much too inviting without paint. He apparently felt responsible for the two of them, but I too had already begun to imagine terrible scenes with them. Some of this stimulated crowd were certainly capable of anything. Jaques opened three different bags and called out to the girls:

"Hold your breath!"

Then he ran towards them quite fast and buried them under a bombastic rain of colour powder. The Indians standing nearby applauded appreciatively. Jacques' theory was correct. Now the two of them looked so upset that they were paid much less attention in the crowd than before. Of course, Jacques hadn't really made himself popular with the crowd. The common colour, which was a blind mixture of most colour powders, was unfortunately something that looked like grey-metallic, and this was soon found all over the body.

Fingernails like a coal miner.

I saw my reflection in a small window a little later. While the colours in the black hair of the Indians were mostly not to be seen, the water bomb in combination with my light hair and the pink powder had done the rest.

I looked like the singer of *Die Prinzen* in his prime. That wouldn't wash out so fast. Alex suddenly stood behind me While on the main street a deafening drumming noise was going on and some dance performance was taking place, he roared into my ear:

"What are you eating?"

"*Bhang Yogurt,*" I pointed to the sign.

Alex's eyes lit up, and after five minutes he came back with two cups.

"*Bhang*" in Sanskrit means *garbage.* This stuff is basically just the rest of the hemp, and therefore not as strong as *ganja* or *charas*!"

So I got another cup. Today was a perfect day to get high. Jaques was more into the rum and chewed some betel nuts in between. I didn't feel any of the bhang at all, and it was only now that I noticed that the yoghurt dealer had set up his stand right in front of the entrance to a small temple. Everyone who bought a cup went to the temple afterwards. The yoghurt was actually nothing more than the traditional ingredient for a religious ritual. Alex and the others wanted to make their way to the campus to clear the buffet. But the temple had a magical attraction for me, so I got rid of my slippers, waved to Alex and went inside.

The Bhang only showed its first effect when I came out of the temple after the half-hour ceremony. I had the feeling that I was able to suck much more air into my lungs than usual when I inhaled. This gave me a feeling of great lightness, floating through the alleys, crossing the main street and finally running to the campus.

Here, like everywhere, all hell broke loose. On the large sports field, about 30 students had flooded a lawn and started playing mud rugby. They slid through the slippery meadow on their stomachs. I had to think of old pictures from the Woodstock festival.

It was already very crowded in the beautiful garden of the deanery. Here, the Holi festival was obviously celebrated in a more dignified way, the professors and doctors of the university were there with their families and celebrated in a row with the students. People wore light-coloured shirts and dabbed themselves lightly and moderately with the bags of paint they had brought with them.

Many buffet tables had been set up under small tent pavilions, and behind each table someone stood to open the food. No doubt all this had cost a lot of money. It was not difficult to spot Alex and Jaques, they stood out from all the others, just like me, because of their enormous smearings of paint. The Greek women stood at the edge and filled water balloons along with smaller children. All in all the party conveyed the feeling of a huge family celebration. The Greek women were weighing two water balloons in their hands and were holding them in front of their chest, giggling, when Jaques rushed towards me and saw that I was watching them.

"Tits don't fall into your hands, you have to earn them!" he said in his French accent and pulled me giggling to the buffet.

Alex was standing at a table with a big bowl. A servant was spooning chai milk into small cups.

"Oh no, that's not Bhang too, is it?"

Alex just nodded happily and said:

"Look around you, today anything is possible!"

His green eyes glowed. Jacques took two cups and gave me one.

"Come on, drink up, or have you just found enlightenment at the temple?"

I satisfied my ever growing hunger with great appetite at the long buffet, while numerous Indian dignitaries of the university hospital were embracing and pictures were taken.

The Bhang made us love the world, for a moment it gave us all the idea of a never-ending summer. We were not too warm, not too cold, not too tired, not too awake. We just felt good.

Rich colors. Laughing people. A temporary Garden of Eden.

Suddenly I felt a hand on my shoulder. A voice was breathing in my ear:

"Oh, Mr. Kemper. How nice to meet you here."

I turned around a little bit slowed down and got scared. It was Ruth Langhans from the institute.

"I see you're making good progress with your research." She brushed across my brow. You could see from her eyes that she had drunk considerable quantities of Bhang.

Again she stroked me, like a little boy, patting my head. I looked around and saw Jacques sitting in the meadow at a distance.

"Have you ever heard of the Lohdi garden, Kemper? We should take a walk there together sometime. What do you think?"

It was too much. I was seized by sheer panic without much delay. I was defenceless against the advances of my almost 60-year-old boss, and all the world around me laughed.

Nevertheless, it cost me some self-control not to laugh out loud, which Mrs Langhans in her condition would certainly have understood as an acceptance of her invitation. I pulled Jacques from the meadow and looked for Alex.

Around 11 pm we came back to the apartment and started to wash off the colours of the day. Banknotes, papers, passport, even my white underpants had been dyed into a light pink, and my hair remained pink even after several washes.

Alex lay on the bed in his underpants and giggled to himself while looking at photos on his digital camera. Then there was a knock at the door.

First I thought it was Jaques and, after knocking several times more violently, it was the drunken Nick. Alex rolled his eyes.

I opened the door.

Outside was Nora.

Alex stood up in amazement. I was speechless. Nora looked infinitely tired. Her clothes were dirty.

"Can I stay with you for a few days?

Osnabrück station, 10:25 pm

I'm a passenger on a miniature model train. It has a strong smell of glue. It gives me a headache. The train passes through some tunnels. On the raw plywood walls inside are obscene words that only I can read. A round through the artificial landscape takes only three minutes. In between, each time we stop at a small station that is supposed to look Bavarian.

At the platform there are little plastic passengers whose feet are standing in small puddles of glue. They are nicely painted, but they have no faces. A figure looks into my compartment with its flesh-coloured face. From a distance I hear a television. The theme song of "Das Aktuelle Sportstudio" sounds softly over. Then the train moves on to the next round.

Goodbye

I could tell right away that Alex liked Nora. For days he was still upset that we had opened the door for Nora in pink underpants. Especially Alex, who didn't care about anything else.

Nora was back.

I told Alex about her. The scarce information had obviously been enough for him to immediately have an idea of who that person was that had wordlessly thrown her blankets on the floor in the middle of the night as a place to sleep.

Alex had offered her his bed several times. Nora refused each time with thanks. We sensed that she was too exhausted to talk. So we didn't ask many questions and let her sleep. Alex lay in his bed, raised his eyebrows and looked over at me. I shrugged my shoulders and turned off the lights.

How had she found us here, and most importantly:

WHY?

Answers to these questions were initially not in sight the next morning. Alex snuck into the clinic and I had to find a quiet corner somewhere to work on the Holi report. Nora was still asleep when we left the room.

Alex walked silently a few meters beside me.

"So this is Nora."

I pressed my lips together and nodded.

"She looks really good. Boy, did she spill her guts to you on that flight."

I just shrugged my shoulders and nodded my head again. Then Alex stopped and looked at me.

"Are you in love with her?"

Immediately I shook my head and gave a decided "Nope" from me.

In love.

I had already asked myself the same question. Somehow I had felt connected to Nora. But that was more because I was taking part in her story. Of course I had interpreted her open manner and her talkativeness as a kind of affection for me. But I had also let myself be touched by other people's fates before, and had not immediately confused love and attachment with each other.

Love, happiness, trust.

What were all those big words. Alex was still silent, and I thought about those big words.

Always, forever.

What actually made it so difficult for me to use such big words, or at least to think about them?

Maybe I just preferred to use the small, the simple and cheap words. They were increasingly difficult and diffuse to define. And that's what made me special. Not having to define myself...

Alex ripped me out of my thoughts.

"We should have dinner with her today. She could probably use some cheering up."

Alex laid out the bait. I knew at first glance that he wanted it so badly. We'd see if Nora got stuck with it.

"Six o'clock at Cafe Raj?"

"You got it..."

It became a rather silent dinner. Alex stared. I was curious when Nora would give him her opinion.

Later, Nora told us that she had found letters at her mother's house.

"Both were actually not addressed to my mother, but to a certain Pantermehl, a friend of my father's in Hamburg. I don't know how she got the letters.

Somehow the name sounded familiar.

"He contacted us from Varanasi in 1986. There he had joined an order.

She took a yellowed and wrinkled envelope from her backpack and read a few lines:

"...I am now a member of the Ramakrishna Mission. Suddenly I'm very respected. People see what I do as representative of themselves. We get charity in return. It's my livelihood. This life seems to have finally come to me. I must judge my success by what I had to give up to achieve it. You know what I had to give up! You saw me in Goa. We both know that there's no greater sacrifice than that..."

Nora put the letter aside and took another piece of paper described.

"This is the last one, from 1992:

...it's time for a new change. I will go north. I will make a pilgrimage to Mount Kailash...

...then even further north, I must find a new purpose. There is said to be a monastery somewhere in the Nubra Valley area that few find and even fewer are admitted to. I will seek it and offer myself there. That will be my destiny. We are only guests on this earth. For several decades... I must use that time to continue to do good. Only by contributing to the happiness of others can I find the meaning of life. That is the meaning. I hope it's not too late for me..."

Alex raised his eyebrows.

"That sounds just like Shangri La!"

Nora and I looked uncomprehending. Alex grinned and explained:

"*Shangri La*. Paradise. A legendary place in Tibet or somewhere up there. It's supposed to be some sort of Garden of Eden. The monks are said to be so healthy they can live well over 100 years. Nature provides them with everything they need. Fertile landscapes, peace, joy, pancakes. That sort of thing."

I thought it was all more than weird and said:

"Do you really think your father gave himself up to this kind of dream dancing?"

Nora looked at me angrily.

"Sorry, I suppose it's possible, considering how upset he must have been when he wrote that."

Nora got even angrier.

I preferred to keep my mouth shut.

Before Nora could start talking to me, Alex had taken a map out of his backpack and spread it out on the floor. I could hardly imagine that, after his own flippant remarks, he took this story of the search for paradise for granted. I got the impression he was just doing it to please Nora. And he succeeded immediately. Nora sat down with Alex and had a more than triumphant expression on her face. She had put the crumpled bundle of envelope on the small table. I took it in my hand, partly out of embarrassment and partly to read the name of the addressee once more. In clear printed letters there was *Hans Panthermehl*, with an address in Hamburg. Even before the feeling from before, when she mentioned the name for the first time, could return, Nora turned around and tore the envelope out of my hand with a spiteful gesture. It all became too stupid for me. For the first time, they made me feel that my presence was disturbing them, I was angry. At Alex, because of his lack of loyalty, and at Nora, because of her stubborn nature. I went jogging.

As I was running, I had a first premonition of the direction in which Nora's arrival would lead the friendship between Alex and me. It was clear that nothing would be as comfortable as it had settled down in the last weeks. I had just got used to my pleasant and orderly everyday life in Delhi.

My premonition was quickly confirmed when I returned after an hour and a half. Nora and Alex were still engrossed in the map. But now they were lying opposite each other on their stomachs, and while Nora followed some routes with her finger, Alex wrote something down on a piece of paper. When I came in, he jumped up and triumphantly held the note under my nose.

"Dude, the three of us should go for a ride!"

I knew it.

Nora looked up briefly.

"Can I talk to you in private for a minute?"

Without waiting for an answer, I pulled Alex by the arm outside the door. Sweating, I stood in front of him and closed the door behind us.

"You can't be serious?"

Alex just looked surprised.

"That woman's hardly been with us a day, and already you let her wrap you up and talk you into some traveling!"

"This was my idea!"

"Oh, nonsense. Your plan is working perfectly. She can't find her father, and then, when the search becomes difficult, she finds someone to pass the time and help her run after this fantasy!"

Like he didn't hear me, Alex started to read me from his note. It was about going to the Himalayas. Nora was really obsessed with the thought that her father was actually still to be found in some monastery up there.

The two had already worked out a complete route. I felt totally taken by surprise and wanted to contradict them. Then Alex put his face very close to mine. I could smell beer on his breath.

"You know, Moritz, life is a rollercoaster, and you're the one who always wants to hold on to something. On the other hand, you're always talking about letting yourself drift. Think about it. All of a sudden this incredible woman is standing here, and we are offered the opportunity to help her. It's like a mission. Don't think about it so much. It could be fate. As long as you don't know what you're doing, you'll do everything right. That's how it always was with me. That's my idea of destiny."

He had looked me firmly in the eye, and even after he stopped speaking, he continued to do so. Then he took a step back again.

I looked at the floor. From inside we heard Nora adjusting the chairs on the balcony. I looked up at Alex again.

"So life is a roller coaster?"

Alex grinned.

"Maybe I should start by putting my hands in the air during the loops..."

Nora was sitting on the balcony. At her feet was a bucket of ice and two beer cans. I sat down beside her. Alex had run off to beg for more beer from Jacques. She handed me one can and cracked the other one herself. For a brief moment it felt like the last few weeks. Why the hell was I only satisfied when I got exactly what I was used to? Hadn't I come to India for exactly the opposite reason? I took a big sip of beer, sat back and cursed my own comfort.

"How did you find us here?"

Nora brushed the hair out of her face.

"I've been asking myself. Mrs. Langhans seems very fond of you. At least she wriggled a lot at first and apparently gave me a fake address for you on purpose."

I couldn't help smiling.

"With a little more charm I went back to the administration department of your institute later and found out that you live in Yusuf Sarai. "Your colleagues are a bit odd, aren't they?"

I nodded because it was true. What was actually keeping me at the institute? Stupid colleagues and a nymphomaniac boss. Maybe nobody would really notice if I went away for a while anyway. I had enough money put aside for a few weeks. Slowly I began to realize that Alex was right. At this point it went on. In a new direction.

When I reached the end of the can, my decision was made.

Bremen station, 11:20 pm

I am leaning against a fast, ivory-coloured sports car standing in the driveway in front of a magnificent estate with a large gate. The ticking of a big old-fashioned cuckoo clock, which is part of the dashboard of the sports car, can be heard exaggeratedly loud. It ticks so loud that it hurts. The sound is driving me crazy. He keeps me waiting on purpose. Then suddenly the cuckoo cries three times and a limousine stops in front of me. The windows are mirrored. The door opens. It's Elvis. He looks beat. His bloated face is smiling at me. Then he throws a gold key ring at my feet and says to me:

"Graceland sucks, I'm not coming back. Watch how you get along here. It's all yours if you want it."

Departure

On Mrs. Langhans' desk was the glass model of a Jaguar E-Type.

I had never cared much for cars, but even I found this one beautiful. It was probably because of its unusual shape. Two-thirds of the car was bonnet, and at the very back there was a driver's cabin with only two seats. The whole thing gave the car something comiclike appearance. It looked both sporty and downright silly. Since I had seen the car in a Helge Schneider film years ago, I thought it was great, and now, sitting in this office, I could hardly take my eyes off it. Whether I officially quit my job or simply stopped coming would probably not have made such a big difference. Probably my disappearance would only have been noticed after one or two weeks anyway.

I had pre-formulated several sentences in my head and wanted to talk about the lack of comradeship in the institute, but when it came down to it, I couldn't think of anything else. She looked at me with big eyes full of expectation, probably thinking that I would come up with a new article or accept her absurd invitation to Lohdi Park.

"I'm quitting now!" was the only thing I could come up with. Then I impulsively grabbed the glass sports car model and said, as I left the office quickly, in a somewhat obstinate voice:

"And I want the car!"

She seemed so surprised by the simultaneity of these two news that she didn't say a word and followed me with big eyes. I could hardly believe myself what I had just done. The glass jaguar weighed heavily in my hand. Actually I was just a thief, but even that felt right at that moment.

The decision for motorcycles was made quickly. However, our exuberance outweighed our decision to go to the Himalayas like in the movie Easy Rider. Nora started to discuss the pros and cons of motorcycles, but in our minds an ideal image was already sparkling: the silly and boyish idea of independence and freedom on chic, shiny motorcycles. We didn't want to let this be spoiled by any discussions.

Fortunately Alex knew a lot about motorcycles. He also had rudimentary knowledge of mechanics, so that we trusted him to recognize the least rough shit in the motorcycle search.

We finally found what we were looking for after four days on the Khari Baoli Road. We had asked ourselves all over the old town until we finally found a wooden crate in a backyard. Sanjeev was the name of the man who wanted to show us two motorcycles. Alex and I stood spellbound before an oily tarpaulin. Sanjeev laboriously removed the cloth. The first impression was positive. I knew immediately, which one I wanted. One second later Alex already said:

"I want the one at the right!"

Fortunately I had chosen the left motorcycle. Alex insisted on test rides with both bikes, so first he rode a lap with our suspicious salesman and then I did. I liked the bike very much. Especially the name had a perfect sound: *Royal Enfield*. Originally a British brand that was still produced in India.

I had only ridden a moped before, but I quickly remembered the gears and the feel of the ride. With the chattering Sanjeev behind me I rode around the block once. The saddle was not too low, you could sit comfortably and reach the handlebars with outstretched arms. The tank was metallic silver and a small leather map folder was attached to it. On both sides there were black saddlebags in the back. I liked the sticker on the speedometer best: *Royal Enfield: Made like a gun.*

After only a few meters I realized that I would need dust goggles. Coughing we returned to the courtyard. Alex already counted off a bundle of rupees. For him money seemed to be no problem at all. Since I had met him, he cheerfully bought what he wanted without paying attention to prices. Now he was going to buy two motorcycles just like that.

Something about Sanjeev didn't appeal to me. Every Indian we'd ever met wanted to trade with us. Bargaining for the price was in their blood, so to speak. Alex spontaneously offered him only half of the price as a start, and we were both more than astonished when he quickly settled for only a little more.

For the same money I had bought a broken moped in Germany when I was fifteen years old, and here we got two Royal Enfields.

Alex drove triumphantly in front of me, and when I tried to turn off at India Gate, I lost sight of him at the roundabout. I stopped at the side of the road. As I looked around, I saw that he did several laps of honor in the roundabout until he finally passed me and patted me on the back of the head. I stepped on the gas and when we came up level, I yelled over to him:

"Were you not surprised by the price?"

He pulled the raised T-shirt off his nose and grinned.

"Why? 500 euros for two stolen bikes is fair.

I felt queasy.

Later he showed me the scratched chassis numbers on the motorcycles, which he said he had seen right at the beginning.

The sun was already setting when we turned into the small alley in Yusuf Sarai. On our faces lay a thin layer of dust.

Nora had made a list of things that could be useful.

At a market, the three of us bought rice, canned food and a bottle of whisky in addition to simple tin cutlery. Nora had found a small shop behind the Connaught Place that sold used trekking boots. Alex and I stocked up there, Nora already had a pair. Bit by bit more and more items collected in a pile in our apartment. In addition to thermos flasks, sleeping bags and camping mats we had to stow away our provisions. Since Nora would be riding the motorcycle with Alex, it was almost clear that most of our wildly mixed equipment had to be stored on my *"Made like a gun bike"*.

It took us a total of five days for the preparations. The longest I had looked for reasonable road maps.

One Saturday night we were sitting together after dinner. I had spread out the maps on the floor and Nora critically studied the route with Alex.

On the card was a small bag of Beedi cigarettes. I had an enormous desire for a short carousel feeling in my head and lit one of them. The problem was that these cheap cigarettes were made from a single thick wrapper with a somewhat crumbly filling. You had to pull much harder on it to get smoke out. As a result, I inhaled much too deeply each time and immediately started coughing. Promptly I got dizzy, I threw the rest of the cigarette on to the balcony. Nora slapped me on the back as I coughed, then I sat down next to them again and bent over the map as well.

I had known that the track would not be a walk in the park, but I only really understood it when I heard Alex reading the altitude data of the mountain passes: up to 5400 meters everything was there.

The next day we were supposed to start.

Fully packed we started early in the morning while it was not yet so hot. We left the congested streets of Delhi behind us. Until noon the area was boring. Fields were lined up one after the other. The eye saw no changes for a while. In the afternoon the landscape changed. There were the first hills, there was blue sky, and the sun shone warmly on our skin.

I had put my headphones in my ears, drove behind them and had no idea what we were letting ourselves in for.

The roads were mostly of quite good quality, and so we made rapid progress on the first day: Meerut, a city of millions north of Delhi, with the oldest church in India, became the place of our first overnight stay. Here the first uprisings against the British colonial masters began in 1857. And this for a very simple reason. The British had introduced new rifles whose cartridges were impregnated with a mixture of beef tallow and lard. To Hindus, cows are sacred. To Muslims, pigs are considered impure. Of course, no British leader had thought of this when the uprising spread like a single wave of violence across the whole country.

Our journey went quickly, but was still not hurried. Nora made a point of covering a certain number of kilometres every day, but at the same time enjoyed it more and more from day to day to spend some free time with Alex and me in the evening. She showed more confidence in Alex every day. And from the third day on the bike she put her hands tightly around Alex's body during the ride instead of holding on to the back of the saddle.

The further we advanced into the north of India, the smaller the cities became. The clouds of exhaust fumes became thinner and the air fresher. In Haridwar we stayed two nights and made an excursion to Rishikesh. Here the Ganges came out of the hills and onto the plain, and as we sat on the riverbank in the evening drinking chai tea, Nora said:

"I can feel that my father was here too."

During the first long stretch I had tried again and again to see this journey as a search. As much as I tried, it felt like an excursion, and I was a participant, nothing else. Alex, who was in love, had quickly internalized the meaning of our expedition. It was easy for him to believe in what Nora hoped to find.

I kept thinking of short episodes from my studies along. A literature seminar in the third semester, during a rainy summer, in which the professor had let us lecture for a whole week on the concept of *hope:* The confidence that something desirable would happen in the future.

"Always remember, people who hope behave positively."

Is that why I was a pessimist? I finished my presentation with the statement: "*Hope is something for people who are ill-informed* and promptly got a D.

On the riverbank some people were sitting and performing their ritual ablutions. We felt that we were in a spiritual place. Maybe Nora's father had really been here. On the other hand, even the Beatles had been here once in the 1970s to meditate.

Alex had put his arm around Nora, and when I heard the first smacking noise behind me, I didn't need to turn around to know what was happening.

Okay. Alex had what he wanted. Did Nora have what she wanted? I suddenly wanted the sauna-flavored taste of a big ice-cold glass of gin and tonic. But instead, the Stones were singing "You can't always get what you want."

Okay.

The next day we made a side trip to the Raji National Park. Alex had complained that he really wanted to see a tiger, and Nora had made up her mind after a short time to do him the favor and granted a tourist highlight as a stopover.

In the afternoon we arrived at the park's front gate and queued up in one of the long lines to get a visitors permit for the Tiger Park.

Nora looked at the sky, and I read an interesting info box about the park in the Lonely Planet. When I looked up, I immediately recognized the disaster.

The third in line before us was Nick.

I tapped Alex on the shoulder and pointed in that direction. Alex flinched, because Nick had seen and recognized us faster than we recognized him. He looked horrible, his face was sunburnt and bloated, all in all as if he had fallen asleep drunk somewhere in the sun.

There was hardly a chance to escape him anywhere around here, so Nick invited himself to join us after a short time. Alex' hatred for him seemed to increase from minute to minute, because Nick could hardly stop staring at Nora all the time from top to bottom, especially at her bottom and her breasts. Nora seemed to be rather unimpressed by this, and so she treated Nick mostly with disdain. Since it was getting late and we all hadn't eaten anything yet, we decided to get the permit the next morning without a long wait and go to a restaurant. Uninvited, Nick came with us.

What a stupid coincidence to run into him of all people in this tourist complex. Later he sat across from the three of us and told us brainless stories, mainly some medical talk. We ordered beer, and Alex demonstratively put his hand on Nora's.

I did not like the situation from the beginning. Nick became more and more aggressive and when his beer didn't come fast enough after dinner, he started to molest the little waiter first in German and then in English. The waiter grinned submissively at first, but after a short while, during which I tried to talk normally only with Nora and Alex, the manager came and asked us to settle the bill and leave his place. I was ashamed and started to dig out my money.

Somehow we had to get rid of Nick.

But suddenly Nick jumped off his chair so quickly that it clattered and fell over, ran towards the boss of the restaurant and screamed:

"I won't pay anything and I'll leave when I want!"

Then he grabbed a bottle of booze from the bar and wanted to go back. Alex and Nora put their jackets on and put money on the table. Nick looked at us wildly, took the small counted bundles of money and held them in the candle flame on the table, then he threw the brightly burning paper money on a plate with leftovers. The whole situation began to escalate. The manager hectically phoned someone on his cell phone, and Nick opened the bootle to take a deep sip and knocked over more chairs.

I couldn't believe we'd get into serious trouble over this guy. Nick started renewed discussions with the manager, and we were just about to leave when another waiter showed up and blocked our way.

Alex pushed him away slightly, took Nora by the hand and went to the door. Tires screeching outside, and I heard excited cries. The police arrived quickly. The tablecloth had caught fire by now and would probably have gone out on the metal table by itself, but it looked threatening. The door opened and six policemen with brown uniforms and bamboo sticks rushed in. A quick discussion broke out between the boss and the police colonel. Waiter and boss complained excitedly about Nick, but also about us.

Nick took a bottle from the table and pushed it lightning fast into the side of one of the policemen. He went completely crazy. Out of the corner of my eye I saw Nora fleeing into a corner while Nick received a full blow to the head with a bamboo stick. Alex was next, and then I felt a pressure on my shoulder and went down. It tickled, then came the pain. I lay on my back and screamed, Nick screamed the loudest. They had thrown him to the floor too, and then three policemen started to kick him.

A policeman started to kick me aside too, and the realization that I would be beaten to death here in some third-rate North Indian restaurant for bilking and disturbing the peace thanks to Nick filled me with horror. I thought I would lose consciousness for a moment, then I was lifted into a car.

At dawn we finally got out of the police station. Nora and Alex had used some persuasion and two thousand rupees to convince the policemen of our innocence in the tumult.

There was no trace of Nick. Maybe they had found drugs on him and had imprisoned him indefinitely somewhere else. Alex looked pretty banged up. There was a small wound on the back of his head, his hair still encrusted with blood. My shoulder hurt. Nora was in surprisingly good spirits. But the good mood didn't last long, because when we turned into the small street where we had left the motorcycles, everything was empty.

The bikes were gone.

All because of that stupid Nick.

Alex screamed, cursed and kicked into the ground until he was enveloped by a cloud of dust. Nora sat down on the side of the road and put her head in her hands. We had only covered three quarters of the distance with the motorcycles. To report the theft to the police would have made no sense. The officers who had arrested us had probably taken the motorcycles themselves immediately afterwards. Of course we could not object to this, after all the bikes were stolen goods.

Actually, we wanted to go to Manali via Kulu, in order to continue from there over the high mountain passes to Leh in the Jammu and Kashmir region.

The dejection was great. We still had some money and some camping equipment, but especially Nora saw her plan as good as destroyed. Actually, more to make some kind of joke to cheer up, I stood at the main road and kept my thumb out. The international hitchhiker's sign. Coincidentally, at that very moment, a truck loaded to the roof and stinking of diesel fumes rumbled around the corner. To Alex and Noras, but most of all to my greatest amazement, the driver stopped immediately.

The truck driver was a relaxed-looking little man, about 40 years old. He wore a towel around his neck, and when he laughed he revealed three enormous gaps in his teeth. He waved at us in a friendly manner. He actually drove the Manali-Leh route and agreed to give us all a lift for 500 rupees.

It was quite a squeeze on the front bench, we stuffed our bags behind the seats. From the elevated place we had a great view over the street. Alex thanked us effusively in Hindi and mentioned our names. Our nice driver was called Vijay. He had furnished his truck like a living room. Colorful, worn blankets lay over the seats, a big radio was next to the gearshift. Most impressive, however, was his small altar next to the dashboard, which he had decorated with all kinds of colourful glittering stuff and a kind of flashing Christmas lights. Vijay did not ask many questions, after a short time we succumbed to the tiredness and the events of the last night and fell fast asleep.

I woke up again because I had a bad headache. The first conscious breath after sleep was a little shock. I had the feeling that any breathing movement, no matter how deep, was not enough to satisfy my sudden hunger for oxygen.

Vijay smiled at me when he saw how much trouble I had breathing. Then he pointed to the sleeping Nora. It looked like she was panting. Alex puffed rather intermittently.

My skull was throbbing. The landscape had changed considerably in a short time. We were already in the middle of the mountains. Like a snake the narrow road wound its way through the rugged landscape. The oncoming traffic could only pass by if you cooperated and drove into small laybys, which had been beaten into the mountain again and again right and left. I asked Vijay how high we might be. He looked concentrated on the road and then held his hand in my direction. He held up four fingers. Then five. We were somewhere between 4000 and 5000 meters above sea level. The view was gigantic, behind every corner a new peak appeared, which seemed to exceed all previous ones in height.

But the best thing about the mountains, the good thing about having come so far up, was that up here the thoughts could move freely in all directions. The air was clear and crisp.

Alex and Nora woke up a few minutes after me. They gave the same spectacle as I had, and this time I could understand that Vijay had laughed. It looked really funny. Alex blew his cheeks open and Nora's nostrils wagged. Vijay drove his load and his three passengers gasping for air like fishes out of the water very reliably over one of the highest drivable mountain passes in the world. But towards evening there was a forced break.

In front of us a small truck had just tipped over backwards in a steep curve. Now a part of the load was rolling down the pass road. The front wheels were completely in the air and still spinning. Since the road was completely blocked, we also got out and helped to collect the scattered load. Most of it consisted of plastic cans, some of which the wind unfortunately blew quickly into the abyss beside the road. Nora and Alex watched the strenuous attempts to stuff more and more people into the driver's cab in order to make the truck in front heavy enough. Nora was fascinated by it.

"Up here, people need each other. You see how they help each other? The mountains are ruthless and sometimes lethal, but they seem to make people more helpful."

Alex nodded to her eagerly.

After all, they had no other choice.

If no one helped, no one would reach their destination.

In the late afternoon we arrived in Leh.

A wonderful little town. On a mountain to the north an old palace was enthroned above the town. From the distance it looked like a small copy of the Potala in Lhasa. The Indus River meandered past the small town. The river, which supplied millions of people with its water and finally gave India its name. We were very close to its origin.

The proximity to Tibet was soon felt. At the same time, unfortunately, also the proximity to the borders of China and Pakistan. Armed soldiers patrolled everywhere. At the gates of the city, the overcrowded Tibetan refugee camps were a reminder of the long-lasting misery of these great people, abused by the Chinese.

When I tried to convert the motorcycle bags into shoulder bags with a newly bought leather strap, I felt a throbbing pain in my forearm. Exactly where the dog bite seemed to have healed quite well, the skin appeared warm and bright red. When Alex looked over my shoulder, I quickly pulled the jacket sleeve back over it.

The people in Leh made a much friendlier impression than in Delhi. Their faces looked very different. Their eyes were big, friendly and curious.

Stupas had been erected on two small peaks nearby, which were connected by a long rope on which colourful prayer flags fluttered. It was suddenly easier to believe that we could find a Shangri La somewhere around here. Despite all the soldiers, Leh radiated a wonderful peace. The climate was crazy. While one's head burned in the sun, one's feet got frostbitten in the shade.

Alex and Nora walked slowly, like an old married couple, in front of me, filtering the air for oxygen with short, heavy breaths.

By the evening we had got ourselves a room in a small guesthouse. It was teeming with cockroaches. Mouse droppings lay on the floor and the mattresses smelled like piss. Nora was in a bad mood. Days before I had noticed that she became tense and increasingly irritable at the thought of possibly facing her father soon. She didn't seem to know how she should feel, or could if our journey would soon reach its destination.

I was tired and already lying in bed when I heard Nora's voice roaring loudly. The night was cold, and the old hostel father had filled two old plastic bottles with hot, boiled water for each of us. I had put one bottle behind my back, the other one on my feet. A cosy warmth surrounded me.

First I pulled my sleeping bag over my ears to be able to fall asleep, it was dark and under the crack of the door only some light came through.

When I heard Alex's voice whispering, I pulled the sleeping bag off my head and listened anyway. They were getting louder and louder, but tried to talk hissing and muffled, thinking they could wake me up.

Alex's voice had the usual enthusiastic tone:

"You should thank him for being here, after all, he's the one who led you here."

"I'm supposed to what? Thank you? We're sitting in the worst shithole I can imagine, and I'm supposed to thank him when I meet him? I'd spit in his face!"

"And then? We're not going to the Himalayas so you can spit in someone's face."

Nora's voice suddenly sounded stubborn.

"Then I would take something from him that meant a lot to him."

"So you want revenge?"

"Yes, I think I want revenge..."

"Maybe you would also be happy that you found him again, and this joy would then make all your anger disappear, maybe you are happy..."

Again a mocking noise came from Nora's mouth. The two of them took a short break, I heard how

Nora's breath was strained, as if she was struggling with tears. Then Alex whispered:

"I believe gratitude and revenge are very similar!"

"Bullshit! For me, gratitude is the greatest possible opposite of revenge!"

"But both are triggered by giving each other something By leaving you, he has given you life as you know it now, have you ever thought about where you might be if he had stayed with you? How do you know you would have been better off? Believe me, I am sure that fate has arranged it right for you, and whether we find your father or not, there is no reason why you should have to think about it now, whether you have to hate him or love him, thank him or take revenge".

"Maybe you are right, but I believe in the motto: give something bad, get something bad back. That's the deal."

"What's the deal?"

"Revenge is the deal."

Alex sighed. I heard him kiss her, and then it got quiet. The breathing sounds of the two slowly became calmer and deeper, only I could not fall asleep anymore. Sleep was offended and took its time. Sleep was hiding behind a large pile of thoughts that I just did not want to think now.

The following afternoon we sat in a small café. The sun was shining brightly. In the shadow of a corner a small television was running.

Breaking news.

The young man behind the counter turned up the volume. Tense silence. Bomb explosions in Varanasi, the holy city. The Hanuman temple destroyed, two more explosions at the train station. Many dead. Images of smoke, debris, ashes and injured people flickered across the small screen. Terror was omnipresent. Nora swallowed, Alex looked at me. Suddenly we all became aware with frightening clarity of what we had gotten ourselves into. The Kashmir and Chinese border conflict was happening right under our noses. At some point it could also affect us.

Alex lit a cigarette. Nora averted her gaze from the TV. Tension was still in the air.

Displacement.

That always helped. Alex stammered away.

"But they're not really after tourists, are they?"

"Sure."

"Sure."

"No, I'm not.

Deceptive silence.

You don't have to travel around the world to realize how blue the sky is.

My last girlfriend had always said that to me when I had wanderlust again and I just wanted to get away. She did not have much understanding for my wanderlust.

Home and safe, warm and dry.

Before I started writing the applications to the Goethe-Institut on the second New Year's Day, she had come to me. A snowy day without hectic, the whole of Germany still sedated with residual alcohol. She only had a thick coat and boots on. Nothing underneath. We slept together three times that night. It felt better than usual. More intense and honest. Without words.

Best going–away present I ever got. With a note on the bathroom shelf.

Sometimes it can be a wonderful stroke of luck if you do not get what you wish for.

Of course I understood what she meant. She had guessed everything in advance. Female intuition. Then why was I here? Looking for something bigger, something I probably didn't even want to find?

Alex ripped me out of my mind circus.

"You won't believe it! They even have a golf course here in Leh!"

I quickly closed the drawers in my head and immediately gave myself back to the beautiful, familiar distraction of Alex and Nora.

"Probably the highest golf course in the world!"

Strictly speaking, the golf course, which was maintained by the Indian army near Leh, had nothing to do with golf. There was no lawn, only nine holes marked with old pennants in a sparsely overgrown wasteland. For a few rupees Nora and Alex had borrowed some balls and clubs. The next morning we set off to hit the balls around the area. At the fifth hole we lost our appetite and marched to a cricket game that was taking place nearby. Finding distraction was very easy. It was a great way to kill time. But still there was an uncertain and often paralyzing tension over everything we did. The destination of this journey was a day's journey away. Behind the military restricted area. Special permissions were available for money, only fast processing could not be afforded here. The bribes were simply too high.

I wake up in a bed in a military training area. All the houses are totally shot up. I look at the blue sky, you can hear birds and the air smells good like spring. Then a general in uniform comes and wants to stick a piece of glass in my back. This is followed by agonizingly long discussions as to why I don't want that to happen. I can persuade the general to leave me alone.

A refrigerator stands next to me as a bedside table, from the cracks in the door runs a brown, viscous sauce. All of a sudden everything is black and white and the same dark sauce is running out of all light sources. From the edges of the sun it slowly drips into my bed. Everything becomes greasy and sticky and the sky gets darker and darker. To avoid getting sticky myself, I jump out of bed and run away.

Forgiveness

The Kardung Pass was 39 kilometres away from Leh. An important military route, on which we moved in the delicate triangle between China, Pakistan and India.

Our travel permits for this restricted area had cost only 100 rupees, but two days had passed before we held the small, greasy piece of paper with a multitude of colourful stamps in our hands.

A jeep with driver slowly took us deeper and deeper into the heart of the Himalayas.

This is the way the world ends.

I sat in front and thought about the evening and the strange atmosphere.

The mountain world swallowed us completely. I hardly dared to look down in the curves. Steep gorges, lots of possibilities for falls and accidents.

The driver asked me several times during the trip whether I had already slept with a woman in India.

I shook my head. He explained that you could only really get to know the country if you had also slept with a local woman. I stubbornly stared out the window.

Finally, after almost four hours, we reached the point where the valley opened up to the observer in its full extent.

I was glad to get out. The conversations on the trip had been very exhausting.

We walked from here on. There was no more road. A gigantic plateau lay before us, an extremely barren landscape, which looked like the surface of the moon. A stone desert, only partly interrupted by large amounts of scree and rock, and bordered by the snow-covered peaks of the Himalayas.

In the distance a slope rose in this landscape, and despite the distance we recognized the outline of the monastery, which nestled itself there like a castle or fortress on the steeper slopes. Like an oasis in the desert, the monastery was surrounded by a fine green seam. If one concentrated on it and squinted to see it more clearly, one had the impression that it would disappear again immediately. With every step we took, it became clearer. On the rock-hard ground a thin variety of grass with sharp-edged and short stalks actually grew. In this wasteland the monastery had a hopeful glimmer.

With all the energy we could summon, we put one foot in front of the other. Panting, sweating and still freezing we covered the distance in about three hours. Finally we stood exhausted at the foot of the monastery.

A winding path meandered up the slope to the entrance. On the side of the path were small prayer shrines, colourful prayer flags fluttered in the wind.

Outside silence. Inside the rush of your own blood in your head.

As we approached the half-open main gate, a friendly looking monk of our age ran towards us. His skin was tanned, he wore the traditional dark red robe. His jacket, on the other hand, was a modern North-

Face fleece jacket of the same colour. Murmuring Tibetan sayings, he put a light-coloured cloth scarf around each of our necks and touched our foreheads with his forehead. Then he showed us the way through a crooked, heavy wooden door, which must be hundreds of years old. He himself went ahead.

The first courtyard was small and narrow. Arranged like a rectangle, it probably served as a forecourt for a further and larger square in its middle. Several closed wooden doors formed the further connection to the monastery.

The monk turned around and greeted us in fluent English. He introduced himself as *Lobsang.* When we gave our names, Lobsang folded each one's hands and eagerly indicated a bow. To my greatest surprise, he did not ask a single question about the reason for our visit. From my point of view, it could not be an everyday occurrence that foreign visitors arrived here, if only because of the extreme remoteness of the monastery. Lobsang apologized briefly and disappeared in to one of the doors, only to return a few minutes later with four small cups and a steaming tin pot. He poured each of us a few sips of the steaming butter tea and instructed us to drink. It tasted extremely salty and had a rancid, greasy aroma. But just one sip made me feel warm and full. Nora and Alex also drank and after the first sips they gave a satisfied sigh.

Nora rummaged through her bag and pulled out her father's photo. While she was holding it under Lobsang's nose, she said:

"Thank you for your hospitality Lobsang. We have come all this way to find this man."

She pointed at the photo.

"This is my father."

Lobsang took the photo, but only touched it with a quick glance, then he gave it back to Nora.

Alex and I looked at him tense.

Lobsang swayed his head back and forth.

"I am very sorry I cannot help you at this moment. I will try to give you all the information I can later."

Nora's disappointment was not to be overlooked. As he collected the cups, he explained, not without excitement in his voice, that we had arrived on a special day.

"I am a monk from Dharamsala and have a special mission in this monastery."

Lobsang turned to go and told us in short sentences that the Rinpoche of the monastery, a high spiritual leader, had died a few weeks ago. He himself had now been called to find the reincarnation of the Rinpoche in a neighbouring area. For weeks he had been searching in small villages and had been looking for boys aged one to one and a half years. One little boy had finally caught his attention. The small one had apparently recognized a prayer chain of the late Rinpoche. Today the day had come when he was to be put to the test again. Today everything revolved around this particular ceremony, at the ending of which he finally invited us to participate.

Nora wanted to refer to the photo again, but Alex gently pressed her hand down and whispered:

"All in good time. We can't disturb them now!"

Nora gave in after a short hesitation. In the meantime I had made myself comfortable on one of the bags and held my arm with the other hand. It throbbed and burned increasingly in the last hours. The pain had spread to the crook of my arm since our last long march. But still I did not want to draw attention to myself. Especially not now.

Lobsang explained that he was the only monk who could speak English with us. Therefore he asked us to wait until the inner courtyard was prepared for the ceremony and he could pick us up.

When it grew dark, the singing of mantras was started in the inner courtyard. The voices of many monks gradually united into a deep and vibrating *"Ooohmm"*.

Prayer drums were beaten. There was a complete silence between the *Ohm*, even the otherwise loud howling wind seemed to hold back for a moment. Then again the silence was broken by the bright sound of bells. As it continued to darken, we recognized the glow of fire under some of the locked doors. When louder voices could be heard again, the door we had been waiting outside for almost three hours opened. Lobsang appeared and gave us a nod. We left our sparse luggage where it was and followed him into the large courtyard, richly lit with torches and butter lamps. Calmly he called for silence with his index finger laid on our lips.

The sight was overwhelming. Under the starry night sky that stretched above our heads, about 50 monks followed the ceremony.

Nora was so excited that she could hardly stand still. Her gaze followed the monks' backs row after row. That was all we could see. Lobsang left us standing and walked sideways a few steps closer to a small table that had been set up in front of the crowd. I recognized some religious objects. There were several prayer drums, small hand bells and prayer chains made of glass beads. An elderly monk with glasses then carried a small boy dressed in dark red, whose head had already been shaved, into the courtyard. Lobsang approached him and greeted him lovingly. The older monk stood at the table with the boy. Even without understanding the spoken words, I could understand that the boy was now again shown objects belonging to the late Rinpoche.

The true incarnation would only reveal and confirm itself when the boy picked out exactly the right ones from the many objects. What at first seemed like innocent gimmicks made the Monks hold their breath when he made his first selection.

I only believed in a coincidence when the boy again chose the right prayer chain. My tension grew, however, when the toddler took the right one out of four prayer drums without hesitation and immediately began to play and make sounds with it in his playful and carefree manner.

Finally, the elderly monk offered the prayer bells for selection. The small boy hesitated. I briefly looked to the side. Alex was spellbound like me. Nora I could see was only waiting for the first possible moment to run forward and see the faces of the monks.

My face was burning. If it was not the heat of the torches that made my head glow, I could only have developed a fever. But I soon put that thought out of my mind again. The boy complained when the drum was taken out of his hand again. But the displeasure turned into a bright, childlike laugh as his little hand circled over the four bells that had been set up. Without really wanting to, I now held my breath. The child's hand remained in the air for a short time and then purposefully reached for a small, simply decorated bell.

When the elderly monk with the glasses immediately shouted out a sentence and turned the young one towards the monks, a loud, excited murmur went through the crowd. Immediately all monks threw themselves on the ground in front of the boy, the newly discovered reincarnation of Rinpoche. Without looking at us, Alex and I kneeled down reflexively.

Only Nora, who had stood between us, did not bend her knees. With a few steps she hurried to a side post of the monastery canopy and stared agitatedly into the crowd.

Lobsang saw Nora and had reached her by the shortest route through the crowd. Some monks turned around irritated. Nora was about to fall into the community of kneeling monks. Loud chants started again.

A gust of wind caused all the torches to flicker, not a few of the smaller lights went out. Lobsang held Nora by the upper arms and pulled her back. While Nora still resisted the strong grip, he carefully laid his head from behind her against her cheek. Even from this distance I could read from his lips the few English words Lobsang spoke in Nora's ear:

"He's not here!"

Silently we waited later for Lobsang to come and tell Nora more. Nora sat sunk down on a few blankets in the corner of a small guest room. She had put her hands over her face. None of us felt able to say anything. Alex found it hard to watch Nora suffer like that. He sat next to her, helpless. I got up and looked out of a narrow window. We were still in a porch of the big monastery. Probably we weren't allowed to go any further inside.

The torches and lights in the courtyard had been extinguished. The bright moon clearly marked the mountain peaks of the Himalayas from the night sky. The whole valley at our feet shone in a silvery light.

"There's something magical about this place."

Alex looked at me in silence.

"Nora, I'm sure your father was very comfortable here. I imagine he really found his Shangri La here."

Nora didn't look up.

Monks had brought us three bowls of tsampa porridge. But none of us felt like eating. My arm burned like fire. The pain was actually only bearable if I held it discreetly with the other hand. My pain killers were also running out. Again it was the wrong time to ask Alex to take another look at my arm.

Lobsang came to us after a few minutes. His face radiated dismay. Then he stood up in front of Nora and folded his hands. In clear English words he spoke the monstrous words into the room.

"He is dead. I am so sorry to tell you."

Nora sat there turned to stone. Alex and I understood what had just been said. Nora shook her head. She opened her mouth wide, and for a short moment it looked as if she couldn't breathe. Even before she could say a word, Lobsang explained in his calm voice that the German monk had been very ill for a long time. A week ago he had died in the monastery and had recently received a funeral with all the dignities and honours of a monk.

The passing away of Nora's father had initially been interpreted as a bad omen in connection with the death of the old Rinpoche. Therefore, the burial of his body had taken place immediately.

Single tears ran over Nora's face, leaving small, clean, vertical lines on her dusty skin.

Nora's father had indeed found his place in this monastery. Whether this secluded place was the paradise he had been looking for, only he could have known for himself.

Alex stared at the ground and tried to put one hand on Nora's shoulder, but she immediately shook it off. My head was throbbing. It seemed like an eternity, during which Nora cried silently, we sat motionless and continued to speak to Lobsang. Suddenly Nora stood up, wiped her face with her sleeve and said in a firm voice:

"Where is he buried?"

Lobsang raised his finger and pointed into the air. Nora asked again:

"No, I mean, where was he buried?"

Lobsang raised his eyebrows slightly, as if he didn't understand exactly what Nora meant by *buried.*

"*Jahtor*", he said briefly and lifted his finger again to point in the air. "A Sky Burial."

Nora pulled up her nose and looked around looking for help.

Alex stood up and nodded at Lobsang. Then he sat down next to Nora again, this time a little closer.

"Nora, he's trying to tell us that your father wasn't buried. He couldn't be buried up here. The ground is just too frosty."

Alex took a deep breath and explained to Nora what, according to Tibetan tradition, the *Jhator was.* My stomach became queasy. For Nora it would be much more difficult to understand. She rubbed her eyes and shook her head repeatedly in disbelief when Alex told her that her father's body had been eaten by birds of prey, following an ancient ritual.

Nora stared silently at the floor and pressed her lips firmly together. Then she said, in a very loud tone:

"I have to see it. I have to see how they did it!"

Apart from the howling wind at the window and the crackling of the fireplace, the room was completely silent.

Lobsang looked at us questioningly. Nora looked us all firmly in the eyes. Alex cleared his throat quietly and broke the silence. After Alex had asked Lobsang, he was silent for a while, then he looked at Nora and nodded his head.

The next morning was cold and the ascent difficult. Lobsang led us to a smaller plateau above the monastery.

Two women and two men stood near some artfully piled up stones. When they saw that we came in company of Lobsang, they nodded at us. On top of the pile of stones a body lay clearly visible, which was covered by a cloth. While Lobsang left us standing, went to the stone altar and pulled away the cloth, one of the relatives took his wife in his arms from behind. We could see how sad they looked. After a few seconds the air was filled with the screeching and crying of numerous vultures. They pecked and pecked so violently at the dead body that parts of it fell to the ground. Nora had immediately turned around and buried her head in Alex's arms. When after almost three minutes there was hardly anything left of the body, she turned around again. The relatives were crying.

Then came a second monk with a leather apron. He was carrying a kind of axe and reminded me a lot of a butcher. He crouched down in front of a stone, the size of a small table, and waited until the remaining bones and skull were brought to him, speaking aloud ceremonial Tibetan sentences. One bone after the other was very finely chopped by him with the axe, then he split the skull, took out the brain and mixed it, together with the flakes of bone, with flour, sugar and butter into a pulp, which was carried back to the stone altar. Immediately, vultures came down from the sky again and ate the remains. I felt the breeze of their large wings clearly on my head. Other vultures were already sitting within reach and had waited patiently until the monk had done his work and then began to eat. When they took off again, small sparrows came and picked up the leftovers.

The small mourning community disintegrated and both couples left in different directions.

Was that the end? Food for the vultures and sparrows. A life of self-sacrifice for others? Even beyond death?

We stood together on a mountain plateau at 5500 meters altitude. I breathed deeper and deeper. The lungs demanded more and more oxygen. But this hunger was not satisfied. Icy wind blew through our faces and through our clothes and felt like knifes on our skin. But when the headaches and the pressure on the chest subsided in between, the nausea went away for a moment, we forgave the landscape, the thin air, the hostile environment. We began to forgive each other our bad sides. Silently and without words an agreement took place here, in the deepest Himalayas. With Nora's mad and furious hope, with Alex's blind infatuation and with my silent helplessness towards life. Difficult journeys open the character of the traveller. I felt almost like Nora's father. A pilgrim who is looking for something and can only find it if he has separated himself from everything known and comfortable before.

I turned to Nora and Alex. Then I reached out to them. Hand in hand, the three of us stumbled down the valley. We held on to each other. Nora in our midst.

She looked disappointed. So did Alex.

I remembered words that my father had said to my mother years ago, at a certain moment.

Disappointments are often more important than success. They show me the right way when the whole illusory world I have built up for so long finally collapses in on itself.

I'm standing in the middle of a desert with high mountains. On the mountains are dead corals and shell fragments. A few 100 meters away from me half of a rusted shipwreck lies in the sand. It's the bottom of a parched ocean. In the sky the sun and two moons can be seen both at the same time and equally bright. My lips are dry. Three zebras appear behind me. As they approach, I see them burning. When the glowing animals have come dangerously close, I start to run away.

In some places the desert sand stops abruptly and deep crevices and ditches gape before me. Before I almost fall into one of the crevices, the burning zebras turn to ashes. A gust of wind spreads the grey dust in the air and into my face.

Cognition

I would have found the way from the station to my apartment even in my sleep. Luckily, it's hardly five minutes on foot. A fine drizzle welcomes me when I come out of the station building. For the first time since the airport I feel a short feeling of joy. But this is quickly replaced by an undefined excitement. I am excited and do not know why. I have missed nothing here, and no one is waiting for me. But it does not feel as if the long journey is finally over. Images of the farewell of Alex and Nora go through my mind.

Alex, who dresses my infected wound and gives me antibiotics. Nora hugging me goodbye. Alex and Nora arm in arm, waving at the airport.

A band is playing through the speakers. Encore before the departure. Sweaty bodies and beer bottles on stage. The audience sings along.

There is much relief for your pain.

There's plenty of room for you

in my cognac heart.

I see the brick houses at the beginning of Willebrandstrasse. The walls aquired some more graffiti on them in the last months.

My apartment is in a large old building on the ground floor. Long corridors with many small one- and two-room apartments. Apart from my neighbour I don't know anybody here. An anonymous living battery, with thin walls between the individual life and

187

destiny units. The neighbour will not be pleased to be rung out of bed at this time of night. But I gave her my key. The door at the main entrance is never locked. In the hallway the light is not working again. A thin glimmer of light at the far end of the corridor bathes everything in a dim mood.

I count the doors to my apartment, go one door further and stop. With my finger already on the bell button, I pause. Light from the last flat at the end of the corridor. I just walk on.

An invisible force pulls me through the open door into the strange apartment. It is completely silent, the air filled with the scent of incense sticks.

In the corner there is an armchair with a cover that looks like the fur of an old, wet dog.

The apartment is furnished in an oriental-asian style. There are some candles burning in coloured glasses on the windowsill. The strong aroma of the incense sticks is numbing.

I turn around and discover the big wall next to me. On the wallpaper, numerous photographs and some newspaper articles have been arranged with pins to form a great work of art. The photos have clearly been taken at many different places in Asia. In the twilight of candlelight they almost always show the same motif: a bearded, thin man. The body is so slim that it almost looks sick. The tendons on collarbones, forearms and feet stand out more than clearly. My tiredness makes me forget any caution.

With my fingers I feel the pictures on the wall, as if I could learn more by touching them.

The apartment door is still open. While my fingers are still on the photos, I look around the room. It is the small apartment of a person who has no great expectations of life. A few pieces of furniture, most of them old and worn out.

There is no TV. In a small kitchenette there is a mug of tea, which is still steaming slightly. The floor is a bit dirty and on a small table next to the armchair there is a cooled pipe in a glass ashtray.

When I look again at the wall with the pictures, an older photo falls down and lands with the picture side down on the floor. A light breeze comes in through the hall, I bend down to pick up the photo and hold it in my hand.

The sound of the front door being closed. Shuffling steps on the floor. My gaze is still directed downwards when two worn out leather low shoes appear before my eyes. Slowly I look up, the smell of cold pipe smoke is intense in the air.

He is hardly taller than me and his look lacks any surprise. There's no horror in it either. The deep-set eyes look calmly, but very attentively at me. The hair is dark brown and so long that it covers the ears. The face is covered with deep wrinkles and thus difficult to assign to a certain age.

I went into his apartment as a stranger and touched his private things. Nothing in his behavior indicates that this particularly disturbs him. I straighten up again, my hand, in which I hold the photo, shakes slightly. He walks past me and takes the teacup out of the kitchen corner, then he looks at me again, pulls the bag out of the cup and casually throws it into the sink.

In this smoky, dream-like apartment, a domino in my head is made to fall by the penetrating gaze of the man in front of me. One stone follows the other, one thought follows the next, and in a few fractions of a second, an infinite number of stones lie in my mind, all mixed up in a single heap. But the chain reaction, the chaotic pile of thoughts that seemingly can no longer be ordered, reveals the name.

Hans Pantermehl.

Almost rudely I hit him:

"You are Hans Pantermehl!"

He sips his cup of tea with composure. Then he looks past me for a moment.

"No, young man, I am not Hans Pantermehl. You seem to be confusing things. But you look as though you've had a long journey. Why don't you sit down and tell me about it?"

"It must be you!"

Without paying any further attention to my words, he starts to prepare a second cup of tea.

"You put a note on your door a few months ago saying you were going away for a long time. I took the liberty of removing it. It sounded like an invitation for burglars."

His words and the sound of a teapot filling with water only penetrate me in a muffled way. I sit down in the armchair exhausted. My excitement only subsides slowly.

Hamburg. India. Hundreds of encounters, thousands of impressions, endless feelings.

I don't know what to do with my thoughts. I think very briefly why coincidences always have to feel a little mysterious or very exciting. It's probably because coincidences give us a brief glimpse of our own ideal of life. That which remains denied to our imagination, we call coincidence.

Smiling, he takes the picture from my hand and carefully hangs it back in the middle of his photo wall. My gaze follows him.

Small, black and white, wrinkled and yellowed.

Another snapshot of a life. One of many. A full-bearded young man with a small woman in torn jeans and an army jacket in front of a tent.

I can really see this. I can touch it. I can actually believe in that.

Thanks

to Thorsten, Henry and Paul.

and

for everything,

to my Linda.

Seven Fates. Seven months. Seven tales. Facing a comet burning above the earth, seven people are confronted with the greatest challenge of their lives: themselves.

"Bevor wir verglühen" is written as great as it is cleverly insane, yet fast, courageous and radical like a Tarantino film, in a clear, poetic, but also modern language that is addictive."

Available in bookshops, at Amazon and tredition.de

paperback 8,90 €; hardcover 18,90 €; ebook 2,99 €

224 pages in german; ISBN 9783749753901

Zeitfracht Medien GmbH
Ferdinand-Jühlke-Straße 7
99095 Erfurt, Deutschland
produktsicherheit@kolibri360.de